THE WINNERS CIRCLE

Also by Christopher Klim, *Everything Burns*

Also by Christopher Klim, *Jesus Lives in Trenton*

Understated humor and lack of pretension lend this wry urban fable undeniable charm. ... Klim's lighthearted entertainment possesses genuine heart.
> —*Booklist*

Klim has a colorful past, and it comes to life in *Jesus Lives in Trenton*, which has an ear for realistic dialogue and an eye for city grit that would make Dashiell Hammett proud.
> —*Philadelphia Weekly*

It all comes together in a compelling and funny new novel called *Jesus Lives in Trenton*.
> —*KYW News Radio Philadelphia*

Christopher Klim is that rare talent who brings characters and stories that resonate with the working class and excite the sensibilities of literary connoisseurs. Maybe he's the New Jersey reincarnation of John Steinbeck ... destined to be quite unique in the pantheon of American novelists.
> —*Robert Gover*, author *Hundred Dollar Misunderstanding*

Boot Means is no ordinary man. ... Klim drew upon his personal experiences to bring Boot Means to life.
> —*The Home News Tribune*

The book is indeed a riotously funny, quick read. It also works on a deeper level, serving as an allegory about man's thirst for grace in a chaotic world.
> —*Time Off*

Jesus Lives in Trenton is laden with laughs, insight and an overflowing abundance of literary skill. Amen.
> —*The Boox Review*

Books by Christopher Klim

FICTION
Jesus Lives in Trenton
Everything Burns
The Winners Circle

NONFICTION
Write to Publish:
Essentials for the Modern Fiction & Memoir Market

JUVENILE FICTION
Firecracker Jones Is On The Case

Get the latest information about
the author and learning programs at:

www.ChristopherKlim.com
www.Write-to-Publish.com
www.WritersNotes.com

THE
WINNERS
CIRCLE

Christopher Klim

Hopewell Publications

THE WINNERS CIRCLE Copyright © 2005 by Christopher Klim.

Published by Hopewell Publications, LLC
PO Box 11, Titusville, NJ 08560-0011 (609) 818-1049

info@HopePubs.com
www.HopePubs.com

Library of Congress Cataloging-in-Publication Data
Klim, Christopher, 1962-
   The winners circle / Christopher Klim.
      p. cm.
   ISBN 1-933435-02-X (alk. paper)
   1. Farmers--Fiction. 2. Millionaires--Fiction.
3. Lottery winners--Fiction. 4. Group psychotherapy--Fiction.
5. Swindlers and swindling--Fiction. I. Title.
   PS3611.L555W56 2005
   813'.6--dc22

                                                    2005009340

First Edition

Printed in the United States of America

CHAPTER 1

RATTLER

For a long time after he struck it rich, Jerry Nearing was haunted by the specter of a rattlesnake. It rose in his dreams, just as it had in real life. He felt its thin white fangs piercing his skin, remaking his life in a million ways. He often snapped forward in bed, draped in a cold sweat, aware that he was alone and with no one to hear the ricochet pace of his heart. But the strange part, the hardest fact for him to reconcile, was that on the afternoon he almost died beside a stinking pile of manure, people called it the luckiest day of his life.

Jerry never recalled feeling lucky or even lucky to be alive. On the day the rattler struck, he awoke quiet and somber, docked by small problems with no easy answers. Icy rain sheeted the old farmhouse windows, and damp air filled his nostrils. He held the nagging feeling that the roof was leaking, but Chelsea had left for work without the slightest remark, and the house lay silent as a corpse. Jerry sat up and perked his ears, listening for the shifts and creaks of his beloved homestead. For most of his life, he felt the urge to set about working, somewhere an unfinished task summoned.

"Good deal," he uttered, celebrating the peace that filled his wife's absence. He'd rather make love to her and stay cuddled up beneath the sheets, but they'd been arguing about the roof again. Chelsea had a habit of harboring a disagreement until it grew legs and became a beast of its own. They both knew they didn't have the money to make repairs, and he grimaced at the thought of going one more round with her.

He slid from bed and followed the steps down. He searched for a disheveled pile of laundry or a mean stack of dirty dishes, an indication that Chelsea still burned. The uneven floorboards skipped beneath his bare feet like Braille. Odd sounds emanated from the kitchen. He found the cabinets ajar and saw his pots sprawled across the floor. His best skillet brimmed with water. Chelsea had trumped the argument, distributing his fine kitchen hardware like old wash buckets to catch the rain.

Water dripped from the ceiling in cold blue lines. A symphony of disapprovals splashed in the pots, the chorus to Chelsea's one-note song. Jerry longed to scale the roof and get to work. He knew how to refinish the floors and repair the pickup truck. He owned the time to attack every task imaginable. When General Motors pink-slipped him, when they shut their doors in Trenton for good, they rewarded his loyalty with an endless string of vacation days, minus the pay.

He closed his eyes. If time was money, why couldn't he barter one for the other? He sent up a wish, a prayer, a plea for a bargain. Let God or the Devil hear him now. He didn't care who seized the deal.

When the storm quit, Jerry put on his rubber fishing boots and drove through Hopewell. He labored all afternoon, stopping at each dung heap on his list. People complained about their crap jobs, but his livelihood relied on it. He sold manure to organic farmers around the county.

His Ford sputtered and stalled in the entrance of Taddler's Horse Center. Jerry gripped the steering wheel, willing the old pickup to the crest of the hill. Gravel crunched beneath the tires. He held his breath, as the truck rolled to a halt.

He opened the door and dropped his boot to the ground. He leaned into the steering wheel, and the truck glided downhill toward the horse stalls, powered by nothing more than gravity. He released the air in his lungs.

Several handlers stood by the huge barn doors. Jerry's window was down, and he heard them mock him. *Let them laugh.* He wasn't stupid. He knew how to assemble a door handle and latch for any late model American car. He used to create entire dashboards from raw materials. He always felt that he could match wits with other people, given the time and opportunity. They would never believe he read Dickens, Jules Verne, and the odd Sherlock Holmes mystery too. They would be amazed when he turned over his engine with a can of aerosol and a cigarette lighter.

The truck stopped behind the main barn, where the wet manure piled above the March snow thaw. He grabbed his pitchfork and wheelbarrow and loaded up. It was the largest mound he'd seen in a while, two truckloads, enough booty to buy a flat of roof shingles and construct a truce at home.

"Good deal." He needed a break like this. Last night, as Chelsea eyeballed him across the dinner table, he sensed the cold, dark silence of her retreat. No conversation. No chitchat about her day. They hadn't made love in a month. He might never view the light of the sun again.

A young woman maneuvered up the dirt path to the barn. She wore bluejeans and a beat-up shearling coat, but it was the foal in her arms that caught Jerry's attention, a gorgeous white-nosed foal with spotted hooves. Its mother whinnied in the paddock, nudging the gate.

Jerry studied the wriggling foal. Horses were pretty smart, naturally honest. They didn't hit you with the mysterious stuff that people carried like baggage in their words and actions. He often watched the trainers work the reins for new riders. It wasn't the horse they taught so much but the person on the horse. The best trainers showed a rider how to read a horse and anticipate its movements. Jerry wanted to train horses too, learn to decode that equine language, but he'd spent fourteen years on the assembly line, since the day he graduated from high school. People thought he did nothing else but shovel shit.

The girl stumbled on a large rock, setting the foal loose. Jerry stepped onto the path and grabbed a fistful of the animal's mane. It felt like straw between his fingers.

The foal twisted its neck, tugging to get free. Jerry gathered its legs in his arms. The animal smelled like damp leather, and a gentle lather greased its neck. It beat its head against Jerry's chest, until it relinquished the fight to his grip.

"Thanks." The girl climbed to her feet, taken aback by Jerry's long shadow cast over her. She dusted off her knees. Both the girl and foal seemed suspicious of Jerry's intentions.

He eased the frightened horse into her arms. The foal had wet his sleeve and the front of his shirt, and the scent of warm urine stung his nose.

Embarrassed, the girl tried to keep her eyes away from the stain on Jerry's clothes. "Sorry about that."

He glanced at his boots—soiled with mud and manure. "I'm used to the smell."

"There's a hose if you need it." She pointed toward the spigot near the barn door. They used it to cool down the horses after a hard run.

"No thanks, I'll shower in my own stall." He waited until she disappeared inside the barn, before changing into his spare flannel.

Jerry emptied the loaded wheelbarrow into the truck. He recalled the struggling foal in his arms. He had control of the animal. Then he remembered Chelsea and his heap of unsolved problems. *Damn GM.* They had run south for cheap wages and a sexy tax deal. They shut the plant and liquidated his future. With a steady job and benefits, he'd start a family. He'd have a baby in his arms. Chelsea would get the family of her dreams. She was made for kids.

He wheeled back to the manure heap. Sweet steam rose in the air like an exotic recipe—ripe and firm with hints of foreign spice. Decomposing manure was a living thing, hosting a city of microorganisms and insects, provoking life wherever it mixed with dirt.

Jerry tensed his arms, absorbed in worry, wishing out loud for a complete solution. He raised his pitchfork and plunged his tool into the mass of horse crap that defined his days.

A nest of rattlesnakes opened up to daylight. Several snakes shook their tails, too many to count. They coiled and cocked their heads. Jerry was mesmerized by their proximity and sound. He never imagined hearing that awful noise up close. It fluttered with an obscene rhythm.

A rattler squirmed on the third prong of his pitchfork, skewered like a worm on a hook, and he chucked his tool aside in repulsion and stepped back.

But a six-footer shot from the pile and broke his skin. The fangs set deep and hard, before disengaging from his leg. His heart jerked in an unfamiliar way. In a spit of time, poison injected into his veins. He'd heard of snake handlers who pulled back before the first strike, but Jerry possessed reflexes of stone.

He limped away, grabbing his pants near the bite. Two pinholes floated on the bunched material. It didn't look that bad, but his pulse raced. Adrenaline mixed with venom. How long did it take? Was it already too late? His brain resembled an unplugged appliance that continued to run on its own. *Get to the truck. Don't fall here. Drive.*

He staggered to his pickup and dropped into the front seat, fumbling for his keys. His leg felt numb. His throat constricted. Was he going to die covered in shit? Had he expected this all along? He considered untying his boots.

A rattlesnake slithered past his tires, shaking its terrible song. His heart jumped higher than before.

The girl emerged from the barn. She gave him a double take, as he slumped in the truck. He felt lightheaded. He wanted to call out, but his lips and tongue tingled. Extreme body parts no longer felt like his own. The tips of his fingers, the touch of his clammy hands felt like rubber.

She stepped toward him, curious, but the snakes circled the mound, squirming like a bundle of rope come alive. She stopped moving and went pale. In Jerry's poisoned brain, she appeared more shocked than he.

How queer it was. Nothing but broken bridges ahead. He metered his diminishing breaths. He felt his life slipping through his palms, as if the rope had always been slipping through and now he'd lost the end of it, felt it whipping away like a snake escaping his grip, a snake that didn't even pause to strike on retreat.

"Watch out," he thought he said. Was he really speaking?

He caught his face in the rearview mirror. The silver glass framed his eyes in the sky, and he squinted. The sun was wrong. It grew larger, expanded. No, it was falling through the clouds. That big yellow ball headed straight for his windshield.

CHAPTER 2

JUST THE TICKET

As Jerry regained his wits, he felt nauseous and sore. He wanted to peel the skin off his face. He found himself lying on a stiff bed in an unfriendly room. Rays of sunlight sliced through the window at a severe angle. Time had rolled backward since he last glanced at the sky.

He tried moving, but his legs and arms gravitated to the sheets. He felt bilious and sapped of strength. A heart monitor pinged beside his bed. Tape and wires clawed at his chest, and a rigid i.v. line stabbed his left wrist. In that pain, the sense of it, he knew he was alive.

Beside the bed, Chelsea was folded into a vinyl chair, like a blonde cat. Her wavy locks fell about her face. She wore her working whites, but her shoes were cast aside, and her stocking feet dangled over the seat. Jerry savored the view: his blonde sexpot nurse, always on call. After a decade of marriage, even half dead, he'd never admit how much this image turned him on.

He watched her yawn. Chelsea had a harelip that was badly repaired as a child. They'd joined the halves and fixed her teeth, but her lip bent upward. The sight of it never looked better.

Chelsea noticed him stirring. "Jerry?" She tossed her copy of *People* magazine aside and leapt to the floor.

Primary emotions controlled him. He didn't speak. He wanted to cry, without knowing why.

She came to him, her hands clutching the bed rail like a ride at a theme park. "Do you feel like a million?"

The question sailed right past him. He glanced out the window, trying to rationalize the time of day. "Shouldn't you be on shift?"

"It's not Friday. It's Sunday."

"Sunday?"

"This isn't Mercer Medical either. It's Princeton Memorial."

"I don't get it," he said but felt the wound gnawing at his leg. He recalled the rattlesnake lunging forward, razor fangs impaling his skin. He shuddered.

She cupped his shoulder, cradling it like the head of an infant. "You almost cashed it in, partner."

He'd never heard her speak like that, but soon, every word between them would form a metaphor for U.S. currency. "I forgot what happened."

"You were delirious when they brought you in."

"There was a rattlesnake."

"It was serious, and the antivenin made things worse. You had an allergic reaction."

"I've been asleep?"

"Since Friday, more or less in and out."

Red scaly patches marred his hands and arms. They traveled into the sleeves of his hospital gown. His skin was on fire, and he started to scratch.

She dropped her hand to his wrist. "Don't itch. It'll just make it worse."

"I can't help it."

"They can give you something for it."

He stared at her face. Her mouth curled in that odd way he'd loved forever, exposing a bank of white teeth. He always saw a little of her teeth, but she rarely let so many of them show. It reminded him of their wedding day. She resonated with the same nervous energy. The dimple pooled in her cheek.

"How long am I in for?" he asked.

"Don't worry about that."

"I want to know."

"When you get out of here, you can take life as you please."

"You don't have to sugar-coat it for me."

"I'm not talking about just next week. I'm talking about every week after that too."

Her tone scared him. He sat up, just to prove himself able, but his head whirled, and his vision blurred. He lay back down.

"Take it slow, Jerry."

"I'm trying."

"Don't force it."

He dug for ideas, hunting for the gems he'd conceived beside the manure heap. "Look, I've been thinking about picking up the horse trade, maybe learn to ride."

"Good plan."

"I can teach. It might change things for us."

"You can buy a whole stable of horses if you want."

"A whole stable?"

"And a ranch to go with it."

He knew what she was doing. They often fantasized out loud. It was their little game. On weekends, they drove his old Ford through the wooded hills of Pleasant Valley and talked up the future. They imagined a better life, casting their wishes into the brilliant canopy of leaves, but in the past few months, they barely spoke, and the truck's reliability was spotty. No spontaneous excursions. Chelsea fumed over his prolonged unemployment—a year and counting. It grounded her plans. It forced her to see a reality that they never dreamed.

"I've been talking with some of my clients," he said. "It's an expensive proposition, but I can learn the ropes and make a go of it."

"It doesn't matter." She fished inside her uniform pocket and retrieved a lottery ticket for the Super Pick Millions. She stuck the blue computer-printed paper in his face. "I found this in your wallet."

Jerry's stomach dropped. She disapproved of his purchases, but it wasn't like her to be sarcastic. He'd been grasping for answers, anything to change his luck. "I'll never buy another."

"Of course you won't."

"Trash it."

"Trash it!?" She leaned over the bed rail, all teeth again. "We hit the big one. Thirty-two million."

"Thirty-two million what?"

"We're rich!"

He laughed. She had to be wrong. It was funny how she included herself in the lottery ticket. As soon as she double-checked the numbers, it'd become his mistake and no one else's.

"Are you sure it's for Friday's drawing?" He'd stashed several tickets in his wallet over the last month. He waited for disappointment to assume her demeanor.

"I've checked this thing at least one hundred times."

"Oh, yeah?"

"I called the phone number a dozen times. It's ours. All ours."

"Are you sure?" He let her run with it. Perhaps it was thousands and not millions. A few thousand seemed like millions to them.

"Didn't you hear me?" She started to whisper. "No one even knows it's us yet."

He recognized her resolve. His wife was thorough if anything. "Just us?" he asked, edging into belief.

"Yes." She returned the ticket to her pocket.

"How much?"

"Thirty-two million," she whispered even lower. Her eyes shifted side to side, as if she and Jerry were under surveillance and secret tax agents might fly from the curtains.

Jerry let the big number bounce inside his head. His brain refused to process it. The heart monitor changed its tune. "Thirty-two?"

"It's more than half of sixty, because you selected the instant payment plan."

He didn't remember doing that. It was something that just happened because he didn't specify. Like the numbers themselves, he took what Mojique at the Seven-Eleven gave him for a dollar. "It's our money?"

"Get it through your thick skull, Jerry Nearing. You almost died a millionaire."

A warm sense of relief washed over him, like when he sunk in a steaming tub after a hard day of shoveling manure. No more arguing over which bills to pay first. Forget the menial jobs. He held still. A mixed cocktail of chemicals passed through his bloodstream. He floated above the mattress, sailing into another dimension.

"I guess I can fix the roof," he finally said.

"Fix the roof?" Chelsea reached up to draw her hair into a ponytail. She fidgeted her hand behind her head. Her blue eyes stared off. She wasn't herself, as if a rattlesnake had bitten her too. "We can hire someone to fix the roof. On second thought, let's sell the dump."

"I thought you wanted the farm?"

"I've changed my mind."

"I know it needs work, but it's our dream house."

She patted her uniform pocket. "That was before this."

He realized she wasn't kidding. He waited for a better explanation, but a nurse stood in the doorway, watching them both, and their dialogue stopped cold.

The attending nurse—shapely with deep-set eyes— stepped forward. She wore bright pink sneakers, which squeaked on the floor. Her nametag read Gina Spagnoli. "I see you're awake."

"He's clear and cognizant," Chelsea said.

"I can't sleep forever," Jerry added.

"I'd stay away from snakes," Nurse Gina said. "Or that might happen for real."

"If this place doesn't kill me first."

"Don't blame us for stepping in a rattlesnake pit." Gina's humor was welcome, the attractive adornment of a young woman without worry. It offset Chelsea's intensity, the missing ingredient in the room.

Jerry relaxed. His arms went limp. The heart monitor assumed another rhythm.

Gina checked his blood pressure. Her hands were cool on Jerry's itchy skin, tiny points of relief. She kept glancing at Chelsea. "Where do you work?"

"Physical therapy."

"Here?"

"No, Mercer."

"Oh." Gina turned away, discounting Chelsea as some people did. It didn't matter that they were both medical professionals. Gina worked in Princeton and probably lived there too. She believed she was better.

At least, Chelsea thought so. She scratched her nose, hooking a finger over her mouth. Jerry recognized her rising insecurity.

"I'll get the doctor." Gina scribbled on his chart. She winked at Jerry before leaving the room.

He felt sleepy. He'd lost his train of thought. He asked Chelsea to draw the curtains and dim the light.

The room smelled sterile and dry. He focused on the farmhouse. There was plenty of room along the south side to attach a baby nursery. They'd bought the place because of the acreage, and the way property values had expanded, they probably couldn't afford to buy it again. "Good deal," he said. He'd finally struck dumb luck. He might tear the house down and start from scratch.

Chelsea buzzed about the room, arranging the chairs, straightening her clothes in the mirror. He watched her through the slits in his eyes. The woman was never at peace. Perhaps the influx of cash would buy her satisfaction in places she never thought possible.

"Chel?"

She didn't hear him, her lips moving, locked in thought.

"Chel?" he said louder. "What's the matter?"

She flopped in the vinyl chair and crossed her legs. "I don't know what to do with myself."

"I can see that." He blamed himself. For a year, he'd worn her to a frazzle—a thread of hope that he doubted still existed. They'd been falling into an endless hole of debt and anxiety. Who knew there was a pile of cash at the bottom?

"I've been pent-up here all weekend," she said.

"Why don't you go home and take a shower?"

"Maybe."

"Pull yourself together for work tomorrow."

"I'm not going in."

"Taking a day off?"

"I quit."

"But you love that job."

"I love vacations too. When's the last time we had one of those?"

His eyes were fully open. He wasn't resting with her like this. He needed to watch her. She might skyrocket to the moon if he didn't maintain his sightlines.

"I just had an idea," she said.

He braced himself. It wasn't like her to make spur of the moment decisions. She blueprinted everything, organized the linen closet like a computer schematic, mapped out shopping trips like military assaults. He saw her on her feet again, pacing. He had the feeling that he'd been asleep for much longer than a single weekend.

"I was thinking," she said.

"I was too. We can start that family, and ..."

She flashed her teeth and gums. "How about a real vacation? I want to see Europe. I want to see Paris in the spring."

CHAPTER 3

THE KING OF HOPEWELL

T he secret was out. People knew about the money. The knowledge lay bare like Chelsea's harelip. Jerry saw it in their eyes. Nurses, orderlies, educated doctors stared at the lucky couple, expecting dollar bills to seep from their pores. Jerry wondered if he shouldn't just start tipping the staff, but he knew Chelsea despised overt public displays. She curled her finger in front of her mouth, like he hadn't seen since high school.

Nurse Gina Spagnoli pushed Jerry's wheelchair toward the lobby of Princeton Memorial. He ignored the people who paused to check him out. Thank God, the hospital banned the press and television cameras. He looked forward to Chelsea and him being shut away on their broken-down farm, with the big black dog and dozens of Osage trees buffering them from the world.

"Where's your wife?" Gina's pink sneakers squeaked on the lobby floor.

"Bringing the truck around front."

"Have you known her long?"

"Yes." Jerry glanced over his shoulder. Gina wore makeup and a gold necklace with blood red stones. She'd taken to visiting his room whenever Chelsea went home. She talked about her skiing trips and her real estate job on the side. He preferred listening to her big time plans, rather than her suggestions of his.

Gina behaved as if her every word needed to find ears. "I think people should have a lot of experiences."

"Chelsea and I grew up together."

"There's been no one else?"

"Just her."

Gina pushed Jerry into the elevator, and they descended the building. He smelled her rosy perfume. Chelsea never wore scents. She jogged several miles a day and was built better than most women, but she loathed the attention wrought from perfume and fancy clothes.

When the doors retracted, the light was dim. Pipes and electric conduit ran along the ceiling. Jerry squinted. It was like a completely different building. "Where are we?"

"The basement."

"Is this the way out?"

"I saw the others staring at you."

"I don't mind," he said, relieved she had the foresight.

"We can take the elevator closest to the front door."

He felt lame. He was strong enough to walk. He wanted to use the steps and sneak out the back door. "You don't have to do this."

"Relax." Gina stopped pushing. She placed her hands on his shoulders and worked her thumbs into his skin.

"What's this?"

"What do you think? You're so tense."

He noticed the kinks in his muscles. Her fingers detailed every knot. He let her hands work their magic, sensing his troubles melt away. Since the moment he'd awoken from the snakebite, he'd been in a haze, as if his body didn't belong to him, as if his thoughts came from someone else. "This is good."

"You have enough to deal with. You shouldn't do this to yourself."

Her fingers crawled along the base of his neck. Goose-bumps rose on his arms. Chelsea was a physical therapist. She was able to do this, but he hesitated to ask.

Gina kneaded the long muscles over his shoulder blades, as if folding and flattening dough. "Good boy."

He felt weird about the basement massage. She was ten years younger, yet handling him like a child.

"Good boy." She returned to his neck, fingering his spine. "It's really been only Chelsea?"

"Yes." His skin felt warm, no more rash yet hot in a good way.

"Don't you regret it?"

"Regret what?" He wondered if they were really talking about him? Their conversations were always about her.

Gina slid over the arm of the chair and onto his lap. Her nose parked inches from his own. She acted natural, continuing her massage, but her uniform blouse was unbuttoned, offering a glimpse of her full chest. Jerry blushed, his face and ears bright with blood. He knew they were crimson red.

"Don't you want to sample more of the world?" she asked.

"Like what?"

"I bet there's a lot you haven't seen."

He shifted his legs, hiding his erection. He was ashamed to be aroused so suddenly. He never generated this affect on women. He wasn't supposed to be desirable. He was married.

"I can be a blonde," she said. "Is that what you like?"

His tongue stuck to the roof of his mouth, unable to form reasonable words. He tried not to breathe. Her warm breath bathed his face.

"I'm younger than her," she said. "Think of me in ten years. I know how to take care of myself."

She slid his hand inside her shirt, forcing it against her chest. Her bra was unsnapped in the front. "I can be better in other ways. Someone in your position ... deserves the best."

He posed like a department store mannequin, staring into her eyes. Her supple breast filled his palm, like a spanking-new car headrest just out of the bag.

She rubbed his chest. "Think of all the things we can do."

"I don't know." His mind gridlocked over the possibilities. Over recent weeks, he'd read about exotic travel, fancy cars, and houses with more staff than family members. Rich men were expected to consume the world and all the women in it. Kings and Presidents swore by it, but he'd loved Chelsea since fifth grade, when they'd stumbled into a beehive and ran screaming across the corn rows of Chesterfield. His love for her was deep enough to swim in. It felt silly to think that way, yet as he watched his friends' marriages dissolve, some more than once, he believed that they never experienced real love. With Chelsea, he'd already won the grand prize.

"I can change the world for you." She kissed him, drawing his bottom lip between her own. "See, my mouth is flawless."

He dropped his lingering hand. He wanted to demean her, erase his pitiful moment of weakness. "What more of the world is there?"

"A whole lot." Gina's eyebrows arched upward, undeterred. She jammed her business card into his shirt pocket and hopped off his lap. She winked like the first time she'd laid eyes on him. "See you around."

She began pushing the wheelchair again.

He shivered once, a tremor from his soul. He hoped she hadn't seen it. He didn't want to her to think she understood him.

Chelsea took the wheel of the old Ford. She drove the back roads to Hopewell, with the pickup sputtering and stalling around the corners. "I hate this truck."

Jerry barely listened. He was shedding the guilt of being with Gina Spagnoli. He sensed the square edges of her business card in his chest pocket. He formed excuses, blaming the ambitious nurse for the encounter. He determined to never tell Chelsea. "What did you say?"

"I can't wait to drive this rusted piece of junk into the river. Why don't we do it this afternoon?"

"We're always going to need a knock-around car."

"We'll buy another knock-around, a brand new one."

"Why waste the money?"

"Oh Jerry, don't be so pedestrian."

The Ford's engine coughed and chopped down the road. Jerry bucked on the tattered bench seat. "Ease off the gas."

"It needs more gas." She pressed the pedal, and the engine died.

They coasted along a bucolic section of Elm Road. Jerry listened to the tires on the asphalt and the wind swooshing through the window vents.

The truck rolled to a halt beside a drainage trench. The brakes squeaked like Gina's shoes.

"Hit the flashers," Jerry said. "We're half in the road."

He left the cab and popped the hood. His arms and legs felt sore; his back too. After more than a week of lying around, he wasn't at full power, yet if he fixed the truck and got them back on the road, his troubles seemed small. It felt good to be working.

The smell of hot engine grime stoked his vigor. He waited for the backfire smoke to clear. He plunged a screwdriver into the carburetor and flipped it open.

The sun baked his head and the back of his neck. He glanced at the windshield to view Chelsea's scowl. He might stand outside all afternoon to avoid another argument.

But they weren't alone. A beige sedan pulled up behind the pickup. Jerry watched two men rise from the front seat. One gripped a camera in his hands.

"Hit the ignition."

Chelsea stuck her head out the window. "What?"

"Turn it over."

The engine moaned and gurgled. Jerry slammed down the hood and shuffled to Chelsea's window. "Slide over."

"You want to drive?"

"There're two reporters behind us." He swung open the door and jumped in. He felt his pulse hitting the mainstream. One of the men raised his camera and snapped a photo.

"Reporters?" Chelsea's voice shrunk.

"That's my guess. They must've followed us from the hospital."

She ducked below the seat. "I don't want my picture in the paper."

Jerry pulled onto the road, spewing black smoke in the men's faces. He watched them in the side mirror. They raced for their car.

"What are you doing?" Chelsea's head was in his lap.

"I'm going to outrun them."

"You're barely going twenty miles per hour."

"It's all the truck'll give me." He checked the mirror. The sedan crawled behind them, caught in a dark cloud. One photographer leaned through the window, but the smoke was too much to bear.

"Here they come." Jerry started to swerve to keep them from passing.

"Stop it." Chelsea rolled onto the floor, smacking her head on the dashboard. "This will never work."

"I won't let them at you."

"You'll have to stop sometime."

He jockeyed the truck. He hadn't thought that far ahead. He focused on their Pleasant Valley home. The reporters might tail them to their front door. "I'm going to lose them."

"Jerry, they're professionals."

He pulled aside to give a pack of cyclists the right of way. A dozen people in helmets and stretchy pants peddled past the Ford, gagging on the fumes.

A man on a dayglo orange bike turned his head toward Jerry. "Get off the road!"

"Is that them?" Chelsea raised her fist above the dashboard. "Paparazzi!"

Jerry floored the gas pedal. The Ford bucked and sputtered, maintaining minimum speed. He fishtailed onto Jacob Johansen's farm.

The tires skipped over the potholes and rocks on the dirt driveway. He noticed the sedan bobbing and weaving behind. The men hopped in the seat, flailing from side to side.

Jerry raced for the house. A thin gray trail spiraled up from the smokehouse. The air smelled like bacon and spent transmission fluid. "We've got them now."

"Got what?" Chelsea braced herself between the dashboard and the floor. She scrunched her face, like a beaver retreating into a hole.

"I can lose them at the creek."

"What are you talking about?"

"Hold on." Jerry wheeled around the barn.

Jacob blocked the middle of the path. The old man stood beside the big plow horse, gripping the bridle reins. His mouth dropped open as if to take in the wind of the approaching vehicle.

The truck was a bullet in slow motion. It bore down on Jacob and the huge horse, wrapped in a shroud of dust and burning oil.

"Shit." He cut the wheel and crashed into the chicken coop, knocking the hen house off its legs. Chickens balked and scattered into the air. Two Rhode Island Reds smacked the windshield and disappeared in a flurry of flapping wings and shooting feathers.

"Oh God," Chelsea wailed, "this is just like Princess Di."

Jerry stayed on the pedal, punching through the coop on the opposite side. Chicken wire folded and scraped over the cab of the truck. He heard Chelsea screaming.

A laying hen danced on the seat, squawking and flapping. "Get it out!" Chelsea said.

Jerry snatched at the excited bird, swerving to avoid a stand of maple trees atop the hill. He glanced in the mirror. The reporters cruised through the scene snapping pictures of the wreckage.

The chicken jumped on Chelsea's back, scratching and pecking. She screamed louder. "Get it off me!"

Jerry pointed the Ford downhill where the path crossed the creek. He leaned over, extending his palm for the bird. It cocked its head to peck, and he throttled the hen in his fist and chucked it out the window.

In the mirror, he watched the bird tumble and right itself. He saw Jacob holding his ground up on the crest. He noticed the sedan rolling downhill in pursuit. "They're still on us."

"Of course they are." Feathers clung to Chelsea's sweater. Bird droppings dotted the seat. She plucked the feathers with the tips of her fingers, as if handling infectious waste.

"Don't worry."

"I'd follow you too." She burned, as mad as he'd ever seen her. "They're waiting to see what you do next."

"Watch me." He hit the brakes, easing into the shallow creek. He knew this trick from years of hunting Jacob's property. Go fast, and you're stuck in the mud.

Water gently slapped the doors of the truck. The sedan gained on them. The truck lifted onto the opposite bank. He crossed his fingers, until the rear tires cleared the water. He paused for a second, preparing the clogged engine for the uphill sprint into the woods.

He nursed the gas, hedging against an untimely stall. The engine whined as it climbed.

The pursuing sedan barreled into the creek, shooting water from its fenders, slowing in the door-high current. Its wheels churned up mud and rocks, until the engine let up a bubbling growl and quit.

The Ford lumbered into the trees. Jerry laughed. "Good deal." For the first time in weeks, months even, he'd done something useful, beat the odds with his own hands.

His wife clutched the seat, less perturbed. She pulled herself straight, assuming the cool demeanor of a woman yanked from the abyss of total embarrassment.

Jerry stuck his head out the window, bending an ear toward the creek below. He didn't notice Chelsea for a moment. He heard two men splashing and cursing in the shallow water. He cut the wheel into the dogwood forest and disappeared into a burst of white flowers and crescent leaves.

At the house, Jerry unleashed Cortez. The massive black dog jumped to his legs and charged onto the property. Its hindquarters disappeared through the spent raspberry thickets, which still poked from the soil like withering finger bones.

Jerry found the old chair in the front room, facing the setting sun. He rested his head against the stained and knotty material and listened to the monotonous gush of running water. Chelsea had gone off to shower and trash her clothes. She didn't bother going upstairs. She stripped in the foyer and jumped in the utility shower on the ground floor.

His nerves were shot, his brain fried. He considered waiting a few hours before driving to Jacob's farm to apologize. He needed to make amends, find a way to repair the car-crashed chicken coop and bruised friendship. But he remembered the money—a trainload of cash heading his way. It still seemed unreal. He'd buy Jacob another coop and all the chickens he wanted.

Jerry went to the cupboard for a drink. He wasn't the hard drinking type. Twice he'd gotten drunk and regretted it—at the prom and on the day GM served him notice. His foreman had stuck a letter in his mail slot, lacking the courage to dismiss him face to face. The boys on the line stood Jerry up at the bar, until he wavered in his work boots. It didn't take long. He had the liver of a five-year-old.

On the shelf, Jerry found an unopened bottle of scotch. He knew little about the varieties of booze, classifying them as either clear or tan. His father was the drinker. He worked in the steel mills in Pennsylvania, phased out during his prime as well. When the old man died, Chelsea sorted through the pitiful items he left behind—a bucket of beer caps, tins of oysters, decks of souvenir playing cards. She kept the bottle of scotch, which Jerry held in his hand. She said it was the best part of him. She said it had aged better than the old man.

Jerry broke the seal and took a sniff. It smelled like dad: strong, abrupt, cured in oak barrels for decades. Dad appreciated good scotch, but he never approved of Chelsea. He only got used to her coming around. Jerry knew it was because of the harelip. What other reason? It was just another excuse for them not to speak.

Ice jingled in an empty tumbler, an echo from Jerry's childhood. He poured a nice amount and took a mouthful of the nasty liquid. It immediately went to his head, and he returned to the lounge chair facing the sun, hoping for the vivid orange rays to glaze his troubles.

Jerry studied his overgrown acreage with the collapsing barn and the weathered farmhouse and its curling clapboard. He finished the drink, letting his mind go fully numb. If he squinted his eyes, he viewed the property exactly as Chelsea intended. Every one of her plans took shape in his head. He decided to begin in the morning.

Chelsea screamed in the bathroom.

Without a thought, Jerry ran. He found her huddled in the corner of the stall. She faced the wall, soapsuds spinning down the drain by her feet. She was naked and dripping wet.

A photographer hovered in the window, but as soon as Jerry filled the doorway, the stranger jumped down. Jerry operated on instinct. His one job in this world was protecting Chelsea. He'd busted a boy's nose in the third grade for poking fun at her lip. He'd thrown another off the high school gym bleachers for the same reason. It was simple. Nobody messed with big Jerry Nearing, therefore nobody picked on Chelsea.

He sprinted to the front porch. He wore sweatpants and tattered sneakers. The afternoon was chilly, and the sun sank on the horizon in a gorgeous purple and pink sky. Jerry noticed none of this. He was fueled by rage and four fingers of scotch—three and one half fingers too many. He retrieved his rusty pitchfork from the side of the house. My property. My right to defend it.

A beige sedan parked at the edge of the woods along the driveway. Jerry marched toward it. The tails of his flannel shirt flapped in the breeze. Where was the dog? He glanced around for signs of life, before sinking the pitchfork into the front left tire.

Chelsea stood on the porch in a towel, her finger curled over her lip. She rarely raised her voice but was screaming for the second time that day. "Are you crazy?"

Jerry braced his heel against the fender, skewering the car again. The opposite front tire collapsed, hissing air.

"Stop it!" Chelsea yelled.

"I am." He knew women didn't like the dirty business in life. That's why they sent men after it, but every time he defended her, she clung to him like a second skin. He knew what she really wanted.

"I'm calling the police."

"That's a good idea."

"Stop! Just stop!"

Jerry spotted the reporters behind a hundred year old oak. The sprawling tree shaded the house but stood apart from the forest. The men couldn't run for cover without being exposed.

He yanked the pitchfork free and cut a straight path for the massive tree trunk.

"No!" Chelsea said. It registered vaguely in his thoughts.

One photographer stepped into the sun with his hands in the air. He wore a black sweatshirt, camouflage pants, and a baseball cap on backward. He fisted several rolls of film, dropping them on the ground. "Take it all."

Jerry gripped the pitchfork. The wooden handle felt warm in his fist.

"Please." The second cameraman had a scarred complexion, readymade for hiding and snooping in the dark. His camera lens poked from his midsection like a weapon of his own. "Take what we have."

Jerry glared at the intruders, raising the pitchfork like a spear. He was Neptune, ruler king, god of the rolling hills of Hopewell. He needed to thrust his mighty tines into their cameras, dispelling reporters from his land forever.

A car horn beeped on the drive. Jerry heard wheels spinning behind him. A black Mercedes raced up and parked shy of the action.

A short man in a suit came out from behind the wheel. He had black hair and silver sideburns. His chin was large and flat, Abraham Lincoln style, a beard of skin and bone.

Jerry glanced between the reporters and the new arrival, unsure of where to launch his first attack.

"Sir?" The stranger paced forward. "I wouldn't do this."

"Why not?" Jerry asked, but the urge to kill dissipated like a static charge. His arms felt drained. He wondered why he'd picked up the pitchfork. It was stupid. He possessed the size and girth to tackle most men with his bare hands.

The stranger stopped walking. "Do it if you want, but it'd be such a waste."

"A waste?"

"Of your options."

Jerry held his ground, struggling for an excuse to back down. What was he doing? He'd toppled the hen house at Jacob's farm and perforated a reporter's car tires like cocktail weenies. Just a few hours outside of the hospital, he'd created a mess of things. He suddenly understood the lives of play-boys and rock stars. His day was in fact material for *The National Inquirer*.

He glanced at the stranger in the double-breasted suit. "Who are you?"

"Haskell Cogdon." He presented his business card—a mini work of art with gold trim and a hologram of his face.

Jerry didn't take it. "Did Chelsea invite you?"

"I'm here on your behalf."

Jerry lowered the pitchfork. He heard sticks breaking in the woods. Cortez materialized in the undergrowth, tongue wagging. Jerry waited for the dog to reach his side. "There you are."

The pure black shepherd nuzzled Jerry's thigh. The dog's fur was soaked and matted and smelled of licorice. Cortez licked Jerry's free hand.

"Been in the creek?" Jerry patted the dog's head. "You should be here when I need you."

The reporters didn't budge. The first man reached for the sky, while the second trembled behind the tree, tossing roles of film around like a sprite dispensing lucky charms. He couldn't possibly have had anything else to give up, but he continued to empty his pockets and tremble. If the oak wasn't as thick as a Roman column, the tree might have been shaking as well.

"You know I mean business." Jerry eyeballed the reporters. "Get the hell off my farm."

Nothing created a better threat than a big man with a huge dog and a sharpened pitchfork. The reporters stumbled for their car and turned over the ignition. They evacuated with such urgency that their car seemed to start before they reached it.

Jerry watched the flopping car tires hit the road. They thumped, spitting an occasional spark as the rims scraped the pavement, but the car plodded along. He waited for it to stumble out of sight.

The soothing sound of the rustling trees resumed. Cortez panted near his feet. Jerry looked toward the porch. Chelsea stood in a towel, hair dripping wet, one arm clutching her robe to her waist. Her free hand was in Haskell Cogdon's hand. She giggled in a girlish way. It reminded Jerry of a scene in a Jane Austen novel, too formal, overdone.

Jerry planted the pitchfork in the cold spring soil. His big toe pushed through the tip of his sneaker. He felt a chill in the air. He ought to run Cogdon off his property too, but he was sliding down the backside of a bad booze high, and the man in the suit appeared harmless. He vowed not to get physical, at least not until sunrise.

Chelsea giggled again. She didn't mind the fresh company, and Jerry refused to argue. That was the biggest thing. With all that money, they didn't need to argue ever again.

CHAPTER 4

A NEW FACE

The money settled in for a few weeks before Jerry and Chelsea drove to a noted plastic surgeon outside of Trenton. Chelsea twisted the Ford's rearview mirror toward the passenger's seat. For days, Jerry found her gazing into anything that caught her reflection.

"It's going to be all right," he said. "Maybe he can do something."

She spun her eyes toward him, without really seeing. "I know he can."

He patted her thigh, tempering her lofty expectations. She'd run this collision course with fate before. As a teenager, she crash-landed a dozen times, drunk on fancy talk from bargain-rate plastic surgeons.

She returned to the mirror. She put her fingers to her face and stretched her cheeks. He watched her create a sleeker mouth—one without the upturn that he adored.

He'd gotten his first glimpse of Chelsea, when they were both six years of age. She was seated in a convertible car. It flew past his house, as he was wandering through the woods, peeling the bark from the birch trees, daydreaming about life before his mother died. The sound of a stock 350 engine roared closer. Jerry stirred from his thoughts and saw Chelsea tearing down the road in that big black car.

Her father drove a convertible Cadillac, like the one in which Kennedy was shot. It had a large open passenger compartment—a rolling upholstered living room. Mr. Adams was an airline pilot, who'd fought in Korea. He arrived home at odd hours and took his only child for wild country spins. Chelsea knelt on the seat, grabbing the air rushing above the windshield. Her hair trailed behind like a golden scarf. Jerry thought he heard her laughing.

The Grolling Egg Farm separated his house from hers. He sometimes glimpsed her from a distance but never up close. She didn't wander away from home. She didn't appear in the supermarket or visit the park. She never came to school, not the first year or the second. Jerry wondered if she wasn't just a girl flying through his imagination, yet she stuck in his mind, like a catchy song lyric, hard to release, hard to keep from playing over and over.

In third grade, Chelsea Adams showed up at Chesterfield Elementary. Jerry heard her name being called, and as she turned to face the class, her future with the kids was doomed at first sight. She'd just finished the last of several operations to join her cleft palate, and a hideous wire assembly strapped her jaw together. It looked moist and red, a gash across the middle of her face. It wasn't the least bit pretty, and the class let her know, gawking, speechless. Sometimes, not uttering a word is worse than a quick and brutal slip of the tongue.

Jerry felt their silent rejection. He knew what it meant to be of no use to people. When his mother had passed away from emphysema, the kids kept their distance from him. He hadn't meant to scare them. He'd only told them how she died. She was eating strawberries when she became violently ill. She collapsed on the bathroom floor, coughing up blood. He thought it was the strawberries. He should've gotten on the phone sooner. Someone—his father, the doctor—needed to know. They called it a tragedy, and his father echoed that thought every day afterward. It was in the way he never really looked Jerry in the eye, the way he swam each night in scotch, bottled himself up along with any decent thought he'd ever had. His father behaved as if he was the only one in the family who had been abandoned.

In school, Jerry and Chelsea didn't speak. They formed islands of uncertainty and hurt. The fall season took hold, and the hardwoods of Chesterfield turned golden brown in the fading light. After class, Jerry used the shortcut through the woods, while Chelsea ran ahead of the others in her yellow dress with the pink flowers. She never talked to anyone. With all that equipment, Jerry wasn't sure if she could utter a word.

It was late October, and plump orange caterpillars clung to the branches and fading foliage. Dried leaves rustled beneath their feet, and the stream rambled over the stones and fallen logs, the dialogue of the forest. Jerry stuck to the path, heading for the large cement drainage pipe that fed the stream. He heard the boys up ahead. Their voices bounced off the water and echoed through the tunnel.

Chelsea stood on the path, staring at the ground. Her knapsack lay in the yellow grass beside her feet.

Peter Kruk and his two pals formed a barricade.

"What's wrong with your face, freak?" Kruk displayed the tight veneer of a kid who'd been whipped too many times by his old man. His jaw jutted forward, and his hands constantly balled into fists. He even wrote with his fingers clenched around a pencil, ready to poke someone that got too close.

Chelsea tried to pass, but Kruk threw his elbow to block her.

"Freak." Kruk laughed, joined by his simpering cronies.

She reached down for her knapsack.

Kruk stamped on the shoulder strap to keep it down. "Where you goin'?"

Jerry ducked into the flagging stalks of dried rushes, waiting for the kids to break up. He was curious too. He wanted a peek at the girl. She excelled at keeping out of people's faces.

She covered her mouth with her hand. Her hair was fastened into a ponytail that curled upon the nape of her neck.

"Can't you speak?" Kruk spit on Chelsea's legs. He was a spitter too, destined for life as a man whom people side-stepped.

Kruk pushed her again, fishing for a reaction to toss in her face. "Speak!"

Jerry heard Chelsea crying. She sobbed, so quietly it hardly rose above the din of the stream. Water swished through the cement tunnel and over a fallen tree. One of the boys plunked stones to the bottom, but Chelsea's whimper wove through it all, penetrating Jerry's ears.

Kruk saw Jerry approaching. "It's the goon."

The insult fell short of wounding Jerry. Kruk said it so many times a day that it was almost funny. Jerry stomped forward. He was taller than the other boys, but he never imagined that he'd silence Kruk until just then.

"The goon and the freak," Kruk barked. "It's an early Halloween party."

Jerry scooped up a stone from the path. The smooth rock tucked into his palm, as if cut to fit. He cocked his arm, taking dead aim on Kruk and his filthy little mouth.

"What you gonna' do?" Kruk puckered to spit.

Jerry saw the moment unfold. Few times in his life, he gained such clarity. His arms and legs moved as if by rote. Chelsea watched from the bank of the stream. He stepped up and thrust his arm forward, stone and all, and slammed his fist on target, knocking Kruk's smart-ass expression out of the exchange.

The punk fell back on his ass—the part of his anatomy that governed most of his thinking. He stared up from the grass, pawing at his face. A trail of saliva leaked from the corner of his mouth. "You, you."

Jerry wasn't the goon anymore. He knew that before Kruk's nose started bleeding, even before Kruk squeezed out dirty tears. Kruk covered his nose and ran, joining his buddies halfway up the trail. Later on, Kruk's father hardly believed that Jerry had fractured the boy's nose, but the kids got the message. Don't mess with Jerry Nearing or anyone who knows him.

Chelsea retrieved her knapsack from the grass and slung it over her shoulder. Jerry watched her turn toward him. She seemed well past crying, collecting herself in a way he would grow accustomed. Her eyes were ice blue, like the color of the sky before it snowed. Her lustrous skin swept away, disappearing into the yellow fur along her hairline. The metal that twisted around her teeth didn't belong to this face. It was no big deal.

"It's okay," she murmured.

Jerry didn't reply. He must have been shaking. He looked past her and down the trail at Kruk's retreat. He felt both scared and proud of the power he'd gained with a single blow.

She nudged his elbow. "We better get home."

They walked for a while in silence. Their feet padded the trail like two young animals. Occasionally their arms touched and pulled back. She mumbled phrases between her wires, and Jerry nodded. She didn't say much beyond 'thank you,' but some contracts are born without even speaking. His job was to shelter Chelsea, and she loved him for it. He was suddenly useful again.

"Open your mouth, please," Dr. Weinberg said.

Jerry watched Chelsea recline on an adjustable chair. They sat in a bright office with budding plants and sculptures with motorized waterfalls. It duplicated the waiting room outside and the offices next door. He felt lost inside a mini-mall for plastic surgery.

"Tilt your head, please." Dr. Saul Weinberg had a patchy gray beard and a body best suited for a lab coat. He passed a lighted magnifying glass over Chelsea's face and furrowed his brow. Haskell Cogdon had recommended Weinberg. Cogdon was making a lot of suggestions, sticking his little fingers into every plan Jerry and Chelsea made.

"Can you do anything?" Jerry leaned forward in his seat across the room. Chelsea wanted a different look. He wanted to restore the farmhouse and purchase a new set of pots and pans. She desired the perfect mouth—a chance to erase her flaw once and for all. A month ago, this wasn't an option, but now they were saddled with options, and Cogdon explored each one, lining their countertops with brochures and prospectuses that supposedly unlocked the secrets of wealth and empire. Chelsea's face seemed the best place to start conquering the world.

"Can you take the ..." Jerry began.

"Give me a minute please," Weinberg said.

Chelsea flinched as the light hit her eyes.

Weinberg folded back her upper lip with his thumbs. "They did a nice job with the teeth. How long ago was this?"

"She was eight during the last operation," Jerry said.

Weinberg ignored Jerry.

"Haskell Cogdon recommended you," Jerry said.

Weinberg returned to his drawing pad. He swept a graphite stick over the paper, scratched his beard, and scribbled some more.

"He claimed you were the best," Jerry said.

Weinberg acknowledged the remark with only a subtle flick of the chin, but when he held up the sketchpad, Chelsea's reaction startled him.

She leapt forward in her seat and embraced the pad in her fists. "Is this me?"

"We can pull down the upper lip and plump the corners," Weinberg said dryly.

Jerry was also shocked by the change. Chelsea had been rendered ordinary by the adjustments on paper. Some men might say beautiful, but she was already the most beautiful woman Jerry knew, inside and out.

"We'll plump the lower to match," Weinberg continued. "You'll be pleased with the result."

Chelsea stared down at the pad, as if gazing into a magic mirror. Jerry wished he knew what she was thinking.

"It's desirable to show some teeth," Weinberg said.

"A little teeth?"

"I call it a Venetian crest. I have photo catalogues for you to browse."

A phone started ringing in the office. After a while, Chelsea and Weinberg were staring at Jerry.

"What?" Jerry said.

"It's you." Chelsea dropped the pad in her lap. "It's the cell phone."

Jerry dug into his jacket pocket. He wasn't comfortable with the device yet. Whenever a phone rang in the past, it typically wasn't for him, even when he used to pray for the job service to call with a prospect. Now he received phone calls day and night. Each call seemed like nonsense, but the nuances of his day suddenly held value to others.

"The green button picks up," Chelsea said.

"Got it." Jerry put the phone to his ear. "Hello?"

"Jerry, my friend." Haskell Cogdon was his upbeat self, ready to ratchet up their lives another notch. He was their attorney, financial advisor, and estate planner rolled into one. Jerry didn't know if they needed that. He only knew Chelsea liked having Haskell around.

"It's Haskell," Jerry called across the room.

"What does he want?" Chelsea said.

"What do you want?" Jerry repeated into the palm-sized device. He felt as if he was talking into a calculator and any minute someone might smirk and hand him the actual phone.

"I have something to show you. I'm coming over." The sound of Haskell's Mercedes hummed in the background. Jerry recognized the ping of the German diesel engine. At the GM plant, if someone drove a foreign car, they had to park in the furthest spot from the entrance.

"I'm not home."

"I know where you are. I'll meet you out front in ten minutes."

"Hello?" Jerry shook the phone and returned it to his ear. "Hello?"

"What did he want?" Chelsea twisted in the chair. She wore capri pants, which exposed a band of skin around her ankles.

"He just hung up."

"That's it?"

"He said he'd be here in ten minutes. He has to show me something, then he hung up."

"And?"

"He just hung up."

"You don't have to say good-bye on cell phones." Chelsea glanced at Weinberg for affirmation. "You just make your point and move on."

Weinberg shrugged. The sleeves of his white coat bunched near his collar.

"What should I do about Haskell?" Jerry asked, confused by the new jargon in his life. It wasn't just the cell phone lingo. He struggled with the terms for their tax shelters and retirement plans, and that literature from Cogdon, which piled in front of their toaster oven, might as well have been pages ripped from a medical journal. A man best suited for machines and power tools felt lame once he acquired the means to employ contractors and lawyers. He suddenly knew very little.

"Go with him?" Chelsea said.

Weinberg nodded, clearly desiring Jerry's absence.

Chelsea turned to the doctor. "We have things to discuss."

"Aren't we about finished?" Jerry asked, but she had that look in her eye, determined, set on a course he'd discover later.

"Go with Haskell. I'll call the car service."

Jerry sunk in the soft leather seat of Haskell Cogdon's Mercedes. They cruised over the pitted back roads of Mercer

County without incident. Blackbirds swarmed overhead. Yanni oozed from the stereo, surrounding the cabin in redundant mellow noise. The car seemed ready to burst into a commercial for itself.

"Did you sign the papers?" Haskell guided the steering wheel with manicured hands. His sunglasses were deep brown, reflecting the sun and the silver shards of hair within his sideburns.

"Which papers?" Jerry sipped a club soda in a crystal glass. A custom mini-bar lay open between the seats.

"If you assign me with power of attorney, I can administer your accounts with better ease."

"So you say."

"One phone call, and I'll do what you ask."

"Can't you do that now?"

"You may miss important opportunities."

"How's that?"

"You might be on vacation, and I can't reach you."

Jerry pulled the cell phone from his pocket. "I thought that's what this was for."

"We'll discuss it again later." Haskell hit the turn signal.

They veered off the main road and into the hills outside Princeton. The pavement disappeared into a narrow path with overgrown tire ruts. A minute earlier, they drove past palatial estates, and the next, they forged deep into a wooded hillside that Jerry never knew existed.

He listened to the sticks and branches snap along the sides of the Mercedes. "You're going to ruin the clear coat finish on this baby."

"The lease is up next month. I'm thinking about a Jag."

"Jag?"

"The sports coup with the convertible roof."

"Chelsea wants one of those."

"I know."

Jerry fidgeted in the seat. He slumped inside smaller cars. He needed more legroom. "Where are we?"

"You'll see." Haskell fixed his permanent smile straight up the path.

They stopped in a clearing dotted with tree stumps. Meadow grass sprouted around the decaying cuts, and early moths flew about the cattails, glittering in the sun.

"Follow me." Haskell left the car. He wore cowboy boots with his double-breasted suit. A scarf poked from his pocket.

Jerry unfolded himself from the car, glad he'd worn his work boots. Chelsea hassled him to update his wardrobe, ordering a fortune in shoes, pants, and shirts from catalogs, but after a cursory look, he let the boxes pile in the corner of their bedroom. He preferred his well-worn boots to the odd Italian loafers with girlie tassels. He favored jeans and flannel shirts over the baggy pants and linen shirts. Forget about the colors. What passed for fashionable and suave would have gotten you beat to a pulp in grammar school, not to mention your stones busted on the assembly line at the car plant.

Haskell led them up a footpath crowded with pine and fir trees with large sticky needles. The attorney stumbled on the big rocks. He wasn't a hiker.

"You want me to carry you?" Jerry joked.

"Wait 'till you see it."

"See what?"

"The view."

"What view?"

"You're a lucky man. People envy a man with options."

Options was one of Haskell's favorite words; mobility too. He spoke like a luxury car brochure. God knows, Jerry'd read enough of them in the last month. He wrestled between the choice of a Land Rover and the super Ford pickup with every amenity. So he asked Ted at the garage to overhaul the old Ford's engine instead. Chelsea still complained about it. "God, we're never getting rid of that bomb, are we?"

When they reached the ridge, Haskell pointed to a flat rock that jutted over the ravine. "Go ahead, there's only room for one."

Jerry stepped onto the precipice without worry. In deer hunting season, he balanced himself on a tree limb for half the morning. He sensed the breeze in his hair and the smell of the budding pines. He loved the woods any time of the year.

"Do you see it?" Haskell asked. "Look through the trees."

Jerry squinted, making out the tops of the buildings below. He recognized an ornate pair of iron gates. The crest held a shield in black and orange. "That's Princeton University."

"Bingo, my friend. B-ingo!"

Jerry glanced back at the little man. "So what?"

"So what?! You can spend the rest of your life over-looking town. That's what."

"Why would I want to do that?"

"Because Chelsea wants it."

"She never ..." Jerry wished he hadn't admitted that. Men will always be men, and he needed to know what his woman wanted before any other man. "I mean, she never mentioned this place in particular."

"She wanted you to see it. It just came on the market. Twenty acres. It's been a tree farm since colonial days."

"What happened to it?"

"The owner died, and the heirs want to sell. Most people don't know about it yet. You have to move quickly."

"I don't want to move."

"Think of the options this place can afford. You can build the house of your desires."

"We're going to do that in Hopewell."

Haskell spread out his arms. "Why Hopewell, when you can have Princeton? At five million, it's a steal."

Jerry fought to stay one step ahead of him. "I suppose you're going to tell me about the tax write-offs."

"Of course."

"Will the soil perk for water and septic?"

Haskell donned a smarmy look, an extension of his repellent persona. "Those are merely details."

Details was another one of Haskell's favorite words, and details were where Haskell would always excel.

Jerry hopped off the rock. He looked down on Haskell. It wasn't unusual for Chelsea to be swayed by dangerous promises, even an intelligent lady like her. Jerry determined to jettison this attorney from his life. He was going to discuss the matter with his wife as soon as he reached home. "Let me think about it."

The lilac sprigs shifted in the breeze, as Jerry drove the old Ford up the drive and past the dilapidated carriage house at the front of the property. Light emanated from the farmhouse, and he spotted Chelsea's silhouette beside the living room reading lamp. The sight of her calmed his nerves. He decided to take the conversation slow. She was a hard mind to change. She trusted Haskell. Jerry wouldn't send Haskell down the block for a loaf of bread. Haskell might not steal their money, but Haskell believed that he knew a better way of spending it.

Jerry tossed his keys and jacket on the chair by the door. He considered dinner, preparing Chelsea's favorite veal dish. "I see you got home alright."

Chelsea never turned around. She perched on the edge of the couch, leaning over a large binder on the coffee table. "What do you think of these?"

He stood over her shoulder, taken aback by the array of photographs upon the page. They were snapshots of naked women, below the chin and above the waist, a full view of bare breasts. "What the hell?"

"What do you like?"

He double-clutched. This was not a question you often answered for your wife, not the typical wife.

She flipped through the pages. He saw round shapes and conical shapes. There were pendulous sacks of female flesh and pairs that stuck out like bookshelves, defying gravity. Some looked petite and pert. Others floated like dirigibles, feminine warships in the sky. He spotted side views and overviews; views of how they'd look lying down. There was nothing erotic about it, just a who's who of breasts in America.

"What are you doing?" Jerry asked.

"I want new ones."

"New what?"

"Breasts, dummy."

He didn't believe it, even as the words left her mouth. Chelsea was a B cup, a nice round shape, still high for thirty-two years. He reached over and slammed the binder shut. "What in the world are you doing?"

"Wouldn't you like more?" She arched her back, pushing out her chest beneath a gray cashmere sweater.

"Did Weinberg suggest this?"

"I asked him."

"Why?"

She led his arm around the couch, until he faced her. "It would be fun, don't you think? Your friends wouldn't be able to keep their eyes off me."

He balked at that. This was a woman who wanted no one's eyes on her. "I have no friends."

"You know what I mean."

"No, I don't."

"Don't be so resistant to change, Jerry. You're becoming a bore."

He took her comment deep. He remembered a guy on the assembly line who chose new breasts for his wife over a pneumatic pump for his garage. He'd bragged to the others that she'd screwed him on the workbench after the operation. The guys laughed. Jerry played along, but he wondered why he didn't want what the others wanted. He believed that if you forced a situation, you ended up with something that you never imagined.

The new grandfather clock chimed the hour. Jerry stared at his wife, flipping through the catalog of breasts again. She was forcing the boundaries of a good thing. It was that damned money. And of course, he'd bought the lottery ticket.

He sat beside her. "I want Cogdon out of our lives."

She looked at him. Her blue eyes swam in the intense halogen light. "I thought we were discussing my breasts."

"I'm done with that."

"This is about the land in Princeton."

"That's another thing. We're not moving. There's no need."

"We can't get rid of Haskell. He's the only man who knows what to do with our money."

Jerry knew she was wrong, but he lacked the vocabulary to defend his point. It wasn't so much his words. He understood the big words. It was the way Haskell presented them. This was another stinging blow to Jerry's ego, and he fell back against the couch. He was aced out of his best role by his own wealth. The skills that had served him well for years were obsolete. Winning the lottery was like being laid-off, except the severance check arrived with a lot more zeros attached.

Chelsea leaned her slender frame upon him. Her forearms propped against his chest. She started with a coy downward gaze, a look that usually melted him to the cushions.

"I know what you need," she said.

He wanted her close. They hadn't made love much. With her not working and an abundance of free time, they were somehow busier. It used to be the one thing they did for free, as often as they liked. He wrapped his arms around her waist. If he held her tonight, everything might be alright.

She started kissing him, unbuttoning his shirt. From the start, they'd anointed her as the aggressor—the one who set the pace. There was nothing better than watching Chelsea strip. He was king of the world.

Her sweater and bra hit the floor. She straddled his legs, undoing his belt.

He examined her chest. The nipples were tight and excited. The size was just right for her proportions. He cupped them in his hands. "You see there's nothing wrong with these."

"You've just gotten use to them."

She reached down to make him erect. She liked to bring him along fast, and then stretch the act out for a long time. He had no other experience with women but heard that they preferred a great deal of stroking and foreplay. Not Chelsea, she wanted him inside her right away, top or bottom, and then she made him work for as long as he hung in there. She wanted him to sweat.

"I like you as you are," he said.

"Things will get better."

"I don't need better."

"You'll see." She dropped between his legs to force the issue. She was ready. He smelled her.

He felt her mouth bring him in, yet his thoughts drifted between her and the touch of her extraordinary lips. He worried about the changes: different mouth, bigger breasts, and God knows what else.

"Jerry?" She looked up from his thighs. She was kneeling on the floor between the coffee table and couch.

"Keep going, honey."

Chelsea went to work again, but the more she tried, the softer he became. "Are you tired?"

"No, no."

"Okay then."

He fought to remain cool, but inside, his thoughts ran wild. His head resembled a lottery machine. Each numbered ball was another lousy notion, bouncing around his brain, fighting to take hold. He'd never, ever done this before. Chelsea always lit his fire. He always delivered.

She used her hand, but his penis grew limp, a completely useless device for the occasion. He heard the grandfather clock chime the half hour. He was losing, and he tried forcing the blood to his groin. Damn, he actually wasn't going to do this.

"Jerry?" She crawled up his to stomach. Her lip curled. "Is everything okay?"

"I'm fine."

"Are you sure?"

He didn't like the tone of her voice, but he didn't look in her eyes. Even though she lay across his stomach, he never felt further away from her. He grabbed onto her shoulder. He tried to recall the first time. He tried to remember it being new again. It was in his head somewhere. Somehow he could reconnect the past to the present.

CHAPTER 5

THE LAST LAUGH

"We need to do more of this." Chelsea held the wheel of her new hunter green Jaguar sport coup. The car emerged from the Holland Tunnel. The burl walnut appointments on the dashboard glowed beneath the overcast summer sky.

"I don't see why?" Jerry was cramped in the passenger's seat, ferreting extra space for his feet and knees. He felt uncomfortable in the baggy pants and sport coat that Chelsea instructed him to wear. He should've put on his old wedding suit and been done with it.

"You promised you wouldn't complain."

"I know." He recalled his last public outing. His former workmates had rushed him into a bar for the afternoon—his least favorite activity. 'You're buying,' they said.

"I want you to mingle." Chelsea checked her hair in the mirror. "These are our peers."

"We've never met them before." He watched her steer onto the Westside Highway. The skyscrapers infringed upon his peripheral vision, slicing it up with towers of stone, steel, and reflective glass.

"It's a party for lottery winners. They're millionaires like us. They have our issues."

He studied her profile. Her lips were plump and sexy, awash in desert rose. Her larger breasts hung firm and high. A black cotton shirt detailed her tight torso. A matching skirt hugged her hips and the sleek contours of her thighs. She'd spent hours with a personal trainer and even more time with a clothes designer and makeup consultant. Jerry feared that merely touching his wife might ruin the finish.

"I'm doing this for you," Jerry said.

"You should be doing it for yourself." She shot a sideways glance, insouciant yet disapproving. She was a living, breathing glamour photo of herself. She'd pulled off the miracle, acquiring the face and body of a star, and she'd done it without him. "Sometimes I worry about you."

He sat up, bumping his head on a rib in the convertible roof. "I've told you one thousand times that I'm alright."

"You've been on the farm for the whole summer. You need to get out."

"I'm out this afternoon."

"Under protest."

"I'm here."

"What would you do if ...?"

He waited for her to finish. He hated when she didn't. It drove him crazy. "What would I do if what?"

"Nothing." She pulled into the barbed-wire parking lot for The Manhattan Cruiser. A hulking orange and blue ferry rocked beside the pier.

"Finish your sentence."

"Don't you have any hobbies?"

She was his hobby. He cooked gourmet meals for her. He managed the farmhouse. "I'm a gentleman farmer."

"Then where are the crops? How about those horses?"

"I'm working on it."

"I thought so."

"What's that mean?"

"Don't sulk, Jerry."

"I'm not sulking."

Chelsea presented their passes to the man at the gate. She tossed the keys to the kid by the valet station, as if she'd done it hundreds of times before.

"Oh no," she said. "Did you pop a pill?"

Jerry rolled down his window. A stale sea odor gusted from the pier. The Hudson River looked gray and choppy, and crests of foam rode the mini swells. "Big boats never make me sick."

"Will you be alright?"

"I'm fine." He'd left his motion pills on the counter at home. He'd have to rough it.

"Do you want to stay ashore?"

He forced a pleasant expression. "I wouldn't miss this for the world."

Pulsating music greeted them as they boarded ship. Jerry disliked loud music and blinked his eyes, barring against the sonic assault. Millionaires churned to a familiar dance tune. They dressed in evening attire. Some were studded in diamonds and gold, as champagne and cocktails drifted past. One man draped his arms around two women. Another staggered from the crowd without shoes. It was two-thirty in the afternoon.

Jerry paused before the extraordinary scene. It was another example of what he'd learned about lottery winners. They owned no sense of time. They weren't bluebloods or corporate raiders with eminent careers and estates to manage. The men and women assembled on the Manhattan Cruiser were dislodged from routine, roaming the planet without a firm agenda. Jerry's buddies on the assembly line used to fantasize about this kind of free time—days filled with nothing better to do than fish, watch ballgames, or hang out in bars—an endless blue collar weekend, only this version had black ties and caviar.

Chelsea's feet moved in a half-strut, already picking up the beat. "This is what I call a party."

Jerry held his tongue. *This is what I call an excuse to leave.*

"I'm going in." She sashayed into the crowd, a flurry of blonde perfection.

He watched her head bob to the music. Men twisted their necks to check her out. They noticed the line of her stockings over her calves and the shape of her tight ass tugging beneath her skirt. He considered joining her on the floor but didn't picture himself inside her halo of glory.

The boat jarred loose from its moorings and coupled with the choppy water. Jerry recovered his balance with a quick sidestep. The stilted peeks of the skyline rolled through the oval portal windows. He felt a twinge in his gut. He grabbed the studded steel post, which supported the upper deck.

Someone was watching. Jerry noticed a man at the next steel post. The stranger came forward. He had short-cropped hair and a pointed nose. He wore a black turtleneck, a tweed sport coat, and precisely creased pants. He dressed like one of the catalogs Chelsea kept flashing in Jerry's face.

Jerry waited to engage the stranger. He'd have to speak with someone at this shindig. He pivoted toward the dance floor to catch Chelsea's eye. He was being a good husband, meeting the other guests, but she was mixing it up herself. She wove in a chain of dancers around the edge of the floor. A man with glasses clutched her hips. He whispered in her ear, and she laughed hysterically.

The man with the short hair held his gaze upon Jerry. "Your first time?"

Jerry prepared for small talk and a quick retreat to the outside railing. "Yes."

"You look new."

Jerry checked his watch. "When do we get back to the dock?"

"I'm with you. This is a bore."

"I didn't say that." Jerry knew he was blowing it. He better summon some charm and pretend he was having a good time. "This is nice."

"This isn't my idea of a party. I come because it keeps me in touch. I get to see who's who."

"So who's who?" Jerry thought he recognized celebrities.

"That's a good question."

"So what's the answer?"

"This party's not for our benefit." The man pointed out the camera crew standing beside the bandstand. "It's a promo for Super Pick Millions. Haven't you seen the commercials?"

"I think so."

"Life's a non-stop party once you win. That's what they're selling." The man looked to the dance floor. Heads shook with the music. Chelsea folded inside the crowd. "If the poor slobs only knew the truth."

The stranger was thinking out loud, and Jerry didn't like it. You shouldn't be inside someone else's head.

"Dick Leigh," the stranger said. "Pleased to meet you."

"Jerry Nearing."

Dick raised his chin. "The pitchfork man?"

It took a moment for Jerry to realize what Dick meant. He recalled the ordeal on the farm during the spring and the awful snapshots in the newspapers. The reporters had smuggled photographs off his property, and the papers mocked him up as a millionaire farmer gone mad—the pitchfork man. "I guess you heard about that."

"I saw it in the news like everyone else."

"It was embarrassing."

"It was great for morale."

Jerry saw Dick's eyes. The fine lines beneath them were smiling.

"We need more of that take charge kind of attitude," Dick said.

"The newspaper almost pressed charges."

"But they used your story instead."

"Right."

"That's what they wanted from the beginning."

"Everyone wants something." Jerry shrugged, wondering what Dick wanted.

"Welcome to the club." Dick shook Jerry's hand. His grip was as intense as his stare. He used it to draw closer to Jerry. "From here on out, hold onto to your wallet."

"So it's like that for you too?"

"I have a buffer." Dick looked past Jerry's shoulder. "You have to be careful. You don't want to end up like him."

Jerry turned and recognized one of the celebrity guests. He was a former NY Yankee who was arrested so many times for cocaine possession that his convictions became a spectator's sport of its own. He was bald now but retained a fresh athletic look, regardless of the endless urine test failures and rehab stints. He was a walking poster child for genetics and strange luck.

"I never use drugs," Jerry said.

"Not him. The chubby man with the dark curly hair coming this way."

Jerry refocused his sights. "I don't know him."

"Tom Veris, a friend of mine. Seven million completely down the drain. One stupid business decision after another."

"I can't imagine that."

"It happens."

"Is he broke?"

"More or less."

Tom arrived holding a vodka tonic and a foaming beer in a tall fluted glass.

Dick snatched both glasses from Tom's grasp. "Do you like beer?"

"Sometimes," Jerry said.

"Do you want something else?"

"This is fine." Jerry accepted the foaming glass, obliging with a sip.

"Wait a minute." Tom's voice was higher than Jerry expected.

Jerry pulled the glass away from his lips. "Is this yours?"

"Why don't you get yourself another?" Dick said.

Tom frowned and retreated to the bar.

"Does Tom work for you?" Jerry asked.

A young man with broad shoulders stood several feet away. His ears curved from the side of his head like satellite dishes. He was listening, snickering at Jerry's questions.

"That's Tucker," Dick said, "my bodyguard."

Tucker nodded to Jerry and then panned a disinterested gaze on the party. He plugged his ears with headphones from a portable stereo. He looked like a Secret Service agent in need of a President.

"Bodyguard?" Jerry asked.

"He's Australian, the best, rugged people. You might think about one for yourself."

"I can handle things."

"That's right. You have that pitchfork."

Jerry wanted to switch the subject. He saw Dick's friend at the bar. "What did Tom do for a living?"

"That's not really discussed here."

"Why not?" *You just told me he blew seven million.*

"If you must know, he owned a bakery."

"What's so secret about that? Isn't it appropriate to know where people come from?"

"We try to forget the past, and you should too. You cashed it in with your first lottery check."

Jerry filed the comment away. Chelsea was forgetting the past. She buried it deeper with each surgical procedure and change of clothes. Every catalog and portfolio that arrived in the mail seemed to cover the past with another disguise. He hardly recognized her, much less saw her around the house.

"There's no looking back once you've won," Dick said. "Even Tom can't. He'd trade a leg to be tossing loaves of bread in the oven again."

Jerry scanned the bandstand. The people on stage were a popular 80's dance group, rendered gray and overweight from the passing decades. They performed a medley of their hit tunes. Jerry struggled to attach a name to the bouncy songs. Why did he ever like them in the first place? Their computerized beats held the appeal and longevity of a paper cup.

"It's like the old adage." Dick stirred the ice in his glass with a plastic cocktail straw. "Even if you stand still, things will change."

Jerry realized Chelsea had vanished from sight. He returned to Dick Leigh, no longer interested in his candor. Why do people with money feel the need to philosophize? Does idle time spawn the illusion of wisdom? "I know things change."

"It's evolution."

The boat swayed in the open harbor. Jerry searched for a distant point to fix his sights, but the skyline undulated in disconcert with his stomach. "I need to get up top for a while. We'll talk later."

"I plan on it."

Jerry checked Dick's neatly groomed facade and set the beer glass on a passing tray. He left without another word.

The dance floor resonated with the heat and smell of millionaires at play. Jerry nudged through the grinding bodies to reach the stairs, but crossing the deck felt like strolling atop the ocean. The boat rode the breakers in the harbor. In the distance, Lady Liberty waved her torch.

Near the stairs, Jerry spotted Haskell Cogdon. His wiry silver sideburns reflected in the portal light. Even indoors, he wore those brown tinted shades.

Haskell snatched a pair of champagne glasses and faded from view. Jerry felt glad that he'd jettisoned that man from his life. People never changed, contrary to Dick Leigh's speculation. Haskell was probably canvassing other suckers at the party.

Jerry climbed to the upper deck. A warm breeze whipped off the Atlantic. He grabbed the railing and aimed his face into the wind. The whitecaps sprayed salty water upon his bare arms and face. He focused on the horizon. The ocean curved off the end of the Earth. He tried to be still inside.

Tom Veris came beside Jerry. His face was tan, plump, and pitted like the head of a bran muffin. Perspiration caught in the dark curls near his forehead. A half-empty glass of beer dangled from the tips of his fat fingers. "So you've met our fearless leader."

"Dick Leigh?" Jerry asked.

"Yeah, he runs the group."

"What group?"

"The Winners Circle."

"Is that what you call this?"

"Not this. It's a chat group."

"You chat about what?"

"Think of it as therapy. We discuss our lives, issues, whatever. Dick's a psychologist. We meet on Tuesdays at the Trenton JCC."

Jerry returned to the horizon, attempting to settle his stomach. He gulped the air. "That explains a lot."

"What does?"

"The shrink part."

"That's just the tip of the iceberg."

"Oh?"

"I suppose Dick didn't say anything about himself."

"He was lecturing me about change." *And spilling your story instead.*

"Change is a big theme lately. I think he's planning something."

"Like what?"

"I don't know yet."

"You two hang around a lot?"

"Dick doesn't have many friends."

Jerry understood that. He used to have friends at the car plant. They used to share lunchtime and talk. You might call it a chat group about cars, home repairs, and sporting events. And Chelsea had her friends, who became his too, but ever since the lottery, things grew weird. People treated them like they were different, special even. He had become alien to familiar places, greeted instead by silence and watchful eyes.

"Dick," Tom continued, "wants to save us all from what he went through."

"What happened to him?"

"After he lost his wife and daughter ..."

"Hold on. How'd that happen?"

"He bought his wife a Lamborghini, and she wracked it up on the Parkway. She and the daughter went with it."

"That's awful."

"Man, you want to know the worst part?"

"What's worse than that?"

"Her remaining family sued her estate."

Jerry wasn't surprised. The closer people came to his money, the more rights they claimed. He recalled standing on Jacob's farm, after he'd knocked down the hen house. He peeled one hundred dollar bills off a big wad of cash, until Jacob's grin split his bearded face in two. "Did her family get the money?"

"Dick fended them off in court. You see his bodyguard?"

"I did."

"Tucker carries a stun gun, not to mention the real thing. Dick told me that Tucker's supposed to zap any family member who closes within ten feet."

Jerry felt ill. Was it Dick's story or the pounding waves against the boat? His stomach surged with every dip. He should've taken a pill. He wasn't going to make it.

"You don't look so good." Tom drained the rest of his beer. Foam limned his upper lip.

"Seasick."

"What are you doing on this tub?"

A shrill of excitement rose from the dance floor, as the boat skipped over a sharp crest. The boat slapped the water. Jerry pressed his fist to his gut, losing confidence in his ability to keep food down. "I don't know."

He pulled away from the railing, the deck swelling beneath his feet. "Where's the men's room?"

Tom seemed to understand motion sickness. The last place you wanted to be was down in the belly of the ship. Tom grimaced an apology, pointing a fat finger downstairs.

Jerry wanted to lean over the rail and purge the limited contents of his stomach, but he considered Chelsea. She'd be mortified if someone saw.

On the stairs, he smelled the millionaires again. The place reeked of expensive cologne, perspiration, and abandoned bites of crab quiche and marinated olives. The air was stagnant, garlicky. It didn't lift or swirl. The dancers stirred up little relief.

He descended into the pit. His stomach gurgled. The boat chopped through the harbor. Few people noticed the sway. They mingled, swinging to the changing rhythm, supporting their bodies on other bodies. Jerry held his breath, hoping to ford the dance floor in time.

The band played 'Gotcha Love'—a hard rocking ballad that failed by any musical standard. Synthesized chords pounded from the big amplifiers, abusing Jerry's unsteady inner ear. He pushed past the dancers and that damned Yankee who was hitting on two women at once.

Jerry gulped the bad air, certain he reflected the color green. The men's room door looked like a submarine hatch, complete with bulkhead and spinning lock. He bore down on the gray steel and pushed inside.

A woman was giggling. Her voice stifled, as soon as Jerry's feet clapped the corrugated metal floor. He paused.

Someone breathed heavily. He saw three urinals, assured he'd located the proper restroom.

The ship pitched and righted. He grabbed the sink, nauseous. But the giggle unnerved him. It was a delicate sound, fluttering deep inside a woman's throat. He knew that sound. It was permanently tattooed upon his brain.

He splashed the faucet in the sink and crept toward the stalls. He heard a man. A couple breathed, moaning softly. Jerry's head spun inside. He crouched down, eyeing the shoes beneath the opening. A cordovan pair of tasseled loafers fumbled with black open toe high heels.

Jerry braced his feet. He felt increasingly ill and dizzy, the essentials of vertigo. The normal reflexes reversed direction in his throat, as blood surged from his head to his gut. He grabbed the stall door with his big hands and yanked with the balance of his power. He wanted to rip the door from its hinges.

The door smacked lamely against the wall. Chelsea sat upon a man's lap, hunched on a toilet seat. Her blouse was unbuttoned to the navel, bra dangling beneath one arm. Her breasts—the gorgeous globes of flesh, which he'd paid ten thousand dollars to enhance—lay exposed to the harsh neon light. Haskell Cogdon's wiry sideburns nuzzled in between.

Chelsea didn't dare move or speak. Cogdon had beady eyes that seemed to expand by the second.

Jerry didn't know where to level his sights. He gazed down at Cogdon's feet. The boat heaved, and his strength escaped him. He clutched the doorway of the stall and vomited on those hideous shoes.

CHAPTER 6

AN OUNCE OF SYMPATHY, A TON OF CHOCOLATE

C ourt papers arrived in a plain brown envelope, via a man with an obvious toupee. Jerry stood on the farmhouse steps, watching the hair hat leave. It disappeared inside a vintage Monte Carlo with a scooped hood. The shiny chrome bumper receded down the driveway.

He tore into the package from Haskell Cogdon's Law Office. It was Chelsea's first communication in almost a month. The last time he'd laid eyes on her, he was fisting the top rail of the Manhattan Cruiser. Rage swirled through his brain, and the remnants of nausea fired his throat. He saw Chelsea sprinting across the parking lot beside the pier. Her long tan legs cut like scissors between the cars. That bastard Cogdon was nowhere in sight.

A strong September breeze rustled the tops of the Osage trees, shaking the plump neon yellow fruit to the ground. Jerry sifted through the crisp legal documents in his hands. CIVIL ACTION FILED IN SUPERIOR COURT OF MERCER COUNTY. Chelsea demanded half of the lottery winnings but passed on the farm. Like GM in Trenton, she was liquidating her position in Hopewell. She salvaged the things she desired, and she abandoned the rest, including Jerry, leaving them to rust beneath the sun. It was pink slip day once again.

For weeks, Jerry prayed for a stalemate. Certified mail from Cogdon's office piled on the kitchen counter, beside dirty dishes and empty cartons from microwave dinners. He spent his days wandering between the porch and the chair facing front. Caterpillars spun silky tents in the pear trees. The cornstalks on Jacob's farm turned golden brown and faded into thin amber husks. Flocks of Canadian geese formed giant V-shapes over the hills.

Jerry watched the last bit of summer wither into fall. His soul grafted to the rotting floorboards and cracked plaster walls of the old farmhouse. He waited, wanting, weary of the silence, unable to grip a notion of a different future.

Whenever gravel churned on the drive, he rushed to the window. He saw the mail truck, the heating oil man, or herds of deer trotting toward the woods. He looked for Chelsea's Jag, the first glimpse of the hydro-mag wheels spinning toward the house. He pictured the top down, her luggage bulging from the trunk, and her blonde hair trailing in the wind.

"This is clever." Ralph Tisch glanced over the court papers from Chelsea's attorney. His head was shaped like an avocado, and wisps of dark hair clung to his feeble chin as if painted in place. He stood behind his desk, surrounded by enough books to crush a healthy man. "It's very clever."

"I'm not surprised." Jerry sat across the room, wondering if anyone really read that many books. They were bound in rich leather, matched sets like collections of encyclopedias. "Her attorney is a sneak."

"Cogdon? He's making it easy for you."

"I don't want it easy."

"Of course you do."

Jerry recalled the last delivery from Cogdon's office. It contained a handwritten note from Chelsea: 'You better deal with this.' He sat forward on the couch. "What's easy about it?"

"A civil annulment erases the marriage."

Jerry sheltered his heart against the suggestion. That wasn't what Chelsea wanted. She was angry for some reason. He just didn't know why.

"Her claim is bogus," Jerry said. "I want children. So does she."

"Where are they? That's what the court will ask. Where are the children? It's the basis of her suit."

"We haven't gotten around to children yet."

"Do you realize how you sound?"

"I'm being honest."

"This woman wants a divorce."

"She's being led on by that Cogdon man."

"She's expediting her departure." Tisch put down the paperwork and cast a staid look on Jerry. "Accept her terms, and you'll have a clean break. Most men would jump at that."

Jerry wondered if they spoke the same language.

"They'll be no recourse in the future," Tisch continued. "Once the paperwork is approved by the courts, she won't be able to make another claim. No alimony. Nothing. Your money will always be yours."

"It's not about the money."

"At this juncture, it's only about the money."

"I want children too. I want them."

"You're missing the point."

"But it's not true."

"What does the truth have to do with this?" Tisch walked around the desk. His long limbs moved with grace, like an alien Jerry'd seen on late night TV, gliding toward its human subject on the examination table.

That's how Jerry felt, strapped down and dissected by strangers with large probing eyes. There were the secretaries with their questions and forms, not to mention Tisch and his legal pad full of scribbled notes. A dry record of Jerry's personal life with Chelsea was being gathered and fed into files and computers for the courts. The emphasis centered on dates, figures, and property—not days, laughter, and memories. It was inhuman, exposing all the wrong parts of their characters.

"Let the case proceed uninterrupted," Tisch continued. "The annulment will come to fruition without a legal battle. It's the smoothest, if not the cheapest path."

"What if I contest?"

"You'll have to answer the primary question in her suit. Where are the children? Their absence strongly supports her argument."

"I can say it's her fault."

"What are you trying to accomplish, Mr. Nearing? That will only drag this out to the same end. Do you understand?"

Jerry refused to understand. Chelsea was confused, her mind clouded by Haskell Cogdon. If Jerry discovered a way to jog her memory, she'd snap out of it and return to him. She used to say, 'There isn't a place in the world for me without you.' How could she forget that? How could anyone?

"I want to talk to her," Jerry said.

Tisch hovered close, his head shifting like a slow motion pendulum. "Mr. Nearing."

Jerry kept waiting for some hideous probe—a jagged spiraling tool—to come whirling toward his brain. He'd wake up without Chelsea, stripped of his memory of the event. "I need more time."

"What do you want me to do?"

"It's a game."

"Excuse me?"

Jerry followed events backward, drawing a line to the instant that Cogdon first set foot on his farm. He'd been a fool to let the little attorney seize the upper hand. Chelsea was his girl. He understood her in ways that Cogdon could never grasp. Life was ideal for her now, but what if things went sour? Who knew her then? He was experienced at lifting her from the hole that she'd inevitably dig for herself.

"Mr. Nearing?" Tisch stopped moving, fazed by Jerry's deep current of thought.

"Let Cogdon try anything he likes."

Jerry stormed from the office. He rushed past the secretary pool and another massive array of books. His heart beat like when he broke Peter Kurt's nose by the creek, but this time, he set his sights on Haskell Cogdon. Let Cogdon come close and—wham—he'd drive the creep to the ground.

Jerry drove to the mall. It was what Chelsea used to do when she wasn't sure what she wanted. Hard rain sheeted his foggy windshield. He parked the Ford beside a fire hydrant, threw on his flashers, and rushed indoors. He hoped for inspiration.

The woman in the chocolate boutique wore a mauve sweater dress with a thick black belt. Her brown hair was separated in a ragged part, and brown locks draped over one eye. It was supposed to be sexy but looked like something out of an old black and white horror flick. "Can I help you?"

Jerry stopped and unzipped his duster. A scrap of paper from Tisch's office stuck to his wet boot. He saw the attorney's raised letterhead. It stoked his will to fight. "Do you have Godiva?"

"Of course." She swept her hand over the gold-trimmed display case between them. "We have truffles and fudge on the back shelf."

"Good." He roamed the golden boxes with ribbons and bows. The smell of the place touched off a memory. It harkened a scent on Chelsea's breath. He used to tuck chocolate kisses in her uniform pocket before she left for work.

"Purchasing early for the holidays?"

"It's for my wife." He clung to the word 'wife' like the final rung of a ladder. The void was widening between Chelsea and him. He needed to close it fast.

"Is there a particular type that she prefers?"

"All of it." He remembered the times that he wanted to buy the best for Chelsea but didn't have the money to waste. The summer ended before he'd gotten the chance to make up for the past.

"I love it too."

"No, I want all of it."

"Every box?"

"Yes. And put aside a three-pound box. I want to take it with me." He had a special plan for that one.

"What do I do with the rest?"

"Can you ship them? I'll give you an address."

"Are you kidding?" She stared, gauging the seriousness of his request, the utter weight of it.

"That's what I said."

"I think we can do it."

"Can you?"

Her spine whipped straight like an old-fashioned car antenna—commission maximus! "You're damned right I can ship it."

Jerry's plan began to gel as he drove to Princeton. He parked outside a string of pricey condominiums near Palmer Square. He saw Chelsea's Aunt Laura walk past the white chiffon curtains of her living room window. She was going to be a hard sell, but he had little choice. His parents were both gone. He had no sisters or brothers to make his case. Forget about asking Chelsea's parents; they didn't return any of his phone calls. He needed a good witness to break up the court proceedings. The cost didn't matter. He needed to buy time.

As Jerry rang the bell, Laura Adams opened the door. She was short but managed to look down on him, observing him like a bruised melon in the market. She didn't like many things. She loathed men, especially her ex-husbands both dead and alive. She reserved her kindest words for wine, opera, and chocolate.

Jerry presented a three-pound box of powdered truffles—the one he'd kept apart from the cocoa tonnage heading toward Chelsea's new address. "How are you, Aunt Laura?"

"Not for long, I hear." Her hair was streaked an unreasonable reddish color. It was an afternoon for bad haircuts.

"I gather you've heard about that. It wasn't my choice."

She fingered the doorknob. "A man who wants to stay married. I'll be damned. What did you do to her?"

He prepared to view a door slamming in his face. He edged his boot tip forward to block. "Can I come in?"

She looked him over again, stopping at his boots. "Take those off."

Jerry undid the laces and took off his work boots. Laura was a neat freak. If he'd thought better, he'd have changed into nicer clothes, opened one of those boxes that Chelsea piled in the corner of their bedroom, taking Laura by surprise in a silk shirt and slacks—the *GQ* man no one ever suspected, even him.

"Are your socks clean?" she asked.

"Yes."

"No holes?"

"Yes." He abandoned his boots beside the door and entered Laura's sterile abode.

The carpet was flat white, as were the walls and Swedish bookshelves. Satin pillows accented the plush off-white couches and chairs. A fluffy cat curled beside a smooth marble sculpture of a woman's torso. Laura bleached the cat's fur at regular intervals. Jerry and Chelsea used to joke about it. It looked like a walking bag of cotton with paws.

"How've you been?" he asked.

"Better than you. You look tired."

"I don't sleep great," he said, but in truth, he slept on and off all day long, just never through the night.

"Do you miss her?"

Jerry set the chocolates on an oriental table beside the door. "Every minute."

"No kidding." Laura sat in a chair by the sliding glass windows. The sun reflected off the marine white deck, adding to the overall brightness of the room.

For a second, Jerry was snow-blind and groped his way to a seat nearby. "Chelsea's filed for divorce."

"No kidding."

"I want to stop it."

"What can I do about it?" She tossed back her shoulders.

He watched her glom onto the moment. She wanted him to grovel. He recalled why he didn't visit her very often. She enjoyed other people's pain, savoring it like a treasured port wine. "Do you remember us in the beginning?"

"You and Chelsea?"

"This isn't easy for me. I wish you'd stop joking."

"Go ahead."

"Did you think we belonged together?"

She didn't answer. Her eyes wandered about the pristine room.

"Chelsea's annulling the marriage," he said. "She's suing on grounds of bearing no children."

"You don't have children."

There she goes, he thought, restating the obvious just like Tisch. "It doesn't matter. She knows I wanted them. You know it too."

"So what."

"Remember that day a couple of years back. You gave us the crib and baby stuff. You said you were never going to need it. It belonged to your mother. I cooked dinner—ravioli and Bolognese sauce. I told you how much we wanted kids."

She bent down to retrieve a scrap of lint from the floor, pinching it inside a tissue. She folded the sides of the tissue over the lint as if wrapping a present. "It's nice to reminisce but ..."

"You have to help. Tell the courts what you know."

"I can't do that to my niece."

"Chelsea's gone mad. I don't know how it happened."

"You must have done something. Did you beat her?"

"Never."

"Drink too much?"

"You know I don't drink."

"Ahh, that's why I don't trust you."

He sensed his blood pressure rising. He tried to look away from her, but she was tossing back her shoulders, pondering the ceiling.

"This is refreshing," she said.

"What is?"

"Now you know how a woman feels."

Christmas passed like the ticking of a clock. New Years too. Each minute separated from the next. He cooked a turkey with sausage stuffing. He watched TV. He stared at that ridiculous log flaming on the tube for hours. He made soup from the turkey bones. A couple of teams played in the Super Bowl, and the same player fumbled twice and blew the game, but Jerry lost track of the score. He kept waiting for camera angles of the fumbler seated alone at the end of the bench.

The sky outside was slate gray for days, but it never snowed. The wind ripped through the barren hardwoods and rattled the skeletal branches and the antique windowpanes. Somewhere along the line, Jerry managed to take his only suit back and forth to the dry cleaners. It was his wedding suit, but court day was coming, and he was going it alone.

Jerry headed for his day of divorce, hardly able to mouth the words. He latched onto phrases like proceeding and dispensation, as if the event had no beginning or end. He drove the Ford out of the hills, descending toward Trenton. His necktie bunched beneath his chin, and his old loafers pinched the broad base of his toes. As he passed Taddler's Horse Center, he glimpsed a man working behind the barn. He hit the brakes and turned around.

The reconditioned Ford lumbered up the incline and past the horse corral. In the old days, people heard the pickup coming down the road, but the man shoveling the manure pile didn't turn his head, until Jerry was almost upon him.

"Morning," Jerry called from the pickup window. He'd noted the mud and filth about his tires and stayed in the truck cab. The last thing he needed was Chelsea spotting dirt on his good shoes. Her sights would drop right to it. She'd almost expect it.

The man wore rubber hip boots and gloves past his elbows. He noticed Jerry's suit and immediately sunk his pitchfork in the ground. "Can I help you?"

"Just passing by."

"Need directions?"

"I used to shovel this same pile."

Yeah right, the man's eyes seemed to say. He propped his hands over the handle and bent one knee, seemingly amused by the attention.

Jerry caught a whiff of the horse dung briefly thawing in winter. It smelled harsh but natural. Not a year earlier, he stood in place of this stranger. He missed the open space and the mix of fresh air and dirt. He longed for the set routine. "Are you selling or taking for yourself?"

"There's an organic farmer in Hunterdon County."

"Hardaway?"

The man seemed reluctant to reveal his client list. "Something like that."

"Better watch out for the snakes."

"What snakes?"

"The rattlesnakes in the pile. If they're still hibernating, they won't like to be woken up early."

The man pulled his tool from the earth. "No snakes in here."

"Oh?"

"They've been cleared out, guaranteed."

"That's what I always thought."

Among the waiting assembly in family court, Chelsea sat toward the front. Jerry spotted her beside Haskell Cogdon. Her blonde hair was clasped with silver combs. She wore a navy blue suit with yellow piping. She looked sharp enough to bring her own caseload before the judge.

She glanced back to the last row. He registered the shock in her eyes. His appearance at the proceedings was optional, and she obviously hadn't expected him. She rose and walked toward the back of the courtroom.

Jerry flipped through the paperwork from Ralph Tisch. He wasn't reading it. He saw nothing but letters and numbers on legal-sized paper. They didn't make sense.

Chelsea came alongside Jerry and sat down. Her silk suit slid across the wooden bench. He shuddered in a private way. They hadn't been this close in months.

"Thanks for the chocolate," she whispered. "I still have a ton."

"I wanted it to last." He'd forgotten about it. He felt stupid all over again.

"I'll never finish it."

He liked the idea of being never completely used up, but he glanced in Haskell's direction and saw the truth of it.

The short attorney scratched his head, trying not to look back.

"Are you still with him?" Jerry asked.

"Don't do this, Jerry."

"He didn't leave with you that day on the boat."

She broke eye contact with him. "I'm sorry about that."

"I looked for him everywhere that day, but I never found him."

"He hid in the engine room of the boat. He bribed the Captain."

"I should have known. He does business that way."

"He thought you were going to kill him."

"It wasn't a bad guess." He'd do it right here, if that's what it took. He waited for an indication, that nervous quiver to her lip. He wanted to touch it, like he'd done many times. He was the first to dare, but now it was beautiful and ordinary. The surgeon had carved out that part of her personality.

Chelsea grabbed his arm, avoiding his glance. A finger pressed the pit of his elbow. Her fingernails were painted French style, peach with white outlines. "You didn't have to come here."

"It's my divorce too. Excuse me, annulment."

"I did it like this so you didn't have to show."

"Do you really want to erase the marriage? Is that what you think of it?"

"It's not that simple."

"I'd rather have a divorce. There'd be a record of us, not this cleaned up effect, Cogdon-style."

She released him. "You're angry with me. It doesn't suit you. It never did."

"I'm better when I have something to fix."

"Jerry, don't screw this up."

"I'm past that point. I'm screwed up already. I want to know what you're doing? That's the question."

She looked at him again. He saw his reflection in her eyes. In many ways, he was the same boy from the woods of Chesterfield, yet she had kicked her life into high gear. She was embarrassed for him. He sensed it down to his core.

"I know you." He saw her as she had been: harelip, normal breasts, regular clothes. She was a terrific therapist, top of her class, but she never missed the details that her egghead college mates disregarded. On Christmas Eve, she stuffed little stockings full of candy and toys for the kids in the neighborhood, and when Jacob Johansen caught a cold, she sent homemade pies and chicken soup. She was the most beautiful person he'd known on the inside. He wondered if she hadn't turned inside out. That transformation was more astounding than anything a plastic surgeon might perform.

"You're making this hard on me," she said.

He appreciated the glint of compassion. He was beginning to think that she'd stowed it away with everything else. "So I'm no good for you any more. Cogdon can do a better job?"

She took his hand in the old way. Her long fingers wrapped over his big hands, hooking over his knuckles. She always set their direction. He was helpless to run against it.

A tear formed in her eye, dangling in the corner. "We have to move on."

Why, he thought but never said it aloud.

The judge slammed down the gavel, dividing Jerry from Chelsea on paper. Jerry left the courthouse. Frozen rain bounced off the steps like fragments from a shattered windshield. He was numb. Rattlesnake venom coursed through his veins. He felt it, tasted it in his mouth. It was pure poison.

CHAPTER 7

THE WINNERS CIRCLE

O n Tuesday nights, The Winners Circle gathered in room 201B at the Trenton JCC. Jerry studied the new faces. They were millionaire winners too. At the first meeting, he'd counted only five heads, yet by spring, a dozen men and women crowded the room. The place held a constant stink of coffee and donuts, and a haze of cigarette smoke hung in the air like the mist at dawn.

"Let's get started." Dick Leigh led the sessions. The Circle was his brainchild. He was a certified psychologist and one of the first big jackpot winners. He dressed in a Gordon Liddy kind of way: sport coats, turtlenecks, hair increasingly shorter. He claimed to have adopted the style during the trial against his dead wife's family. "Can we take our seats?"

Tucker, Dick's bodyguard, assumed his customary position outside the circle of chairs. He leaned against the wall beside the kitchenette counter, digging jellybeans from the pocket of a kelly green windbreaker. The leather strap of his gun holster peeked beneath the nylon zipper. "Coffee's ready."

"Did you use the French roast?" A bald man called over from the chairs. Jerry hadn't learned his name yet.

"Yes." Tucker replied.

"I brought it back from Provence. I hope everyone likes it."

"Smells good."

"I found it in a charming cafe by the sea."

People politely acknowledged the offering.

"Next time," he said. "I'll bring china cups."

Jerry filled a styrofoam cup, like the others. The Circle broke the monotony in his routine. The company wasn't bad either. He didn't have to speak. He needed to have good ears and loads of patience for this crowd. He used to practice those skills with Chelsea, and now the silence at home was killing him.

Tom Veris lingered by the pastry tray, a dusting of powdered sugar on his lips. His sweater bulged at his waistline. "Try the Linzer Tort."

"No, thanks."

"Donut?"

"I'm okay."

"You never eat the donuts, man. It's un-American."

"I used to bake on Sundays."

Tom dangled a jellyroll slice in the air, stopping mid-chew. "You did?"

"I don't have the patience for the measuring anymore." Jerry listened to his own words. A man's typical excuse for being impatient was a lack of time, but for Jerry, time piled up at home like old newspapers, yet he didn't seem to have the patience for making even a simple meal.

A crumb tumbled from Tom's mouth and caught on the shelf of his protruding gut. "That's the beauty of baking. You measure, and it comes out just right every time."

"And if you don't concentrate, you screw up. Table-spoons look like teaspoons, and so on."

Dick turned from the circle. "Are you men joining us?"

Tom and Jerry returned to their chairs.

Dick checked his notes for an opening quote. He liked American Indian logic. He used to recite the Prayer of Saint Francis—something about giving yourself up to God and the will of things—but people asked Dick to stop. One woman admitted that she had enough money to buy and sell free will.

"We are all poor because we are all honest," Dick said. "That was Red Dog, an Oglala Sioux."

During the minute of silence, Jerry considered the quote. Dick was proud of it. Jerry thought Dick was full of horse manure—stacked higher and deeper than any mound Jerry had plied with a pitchfork.

"Who wants to start?" Dick searched their faces.

Arlene spoke first. She was a mutable woman with a permanent tan. She smoked Virginia Slims halfway down and stubbed them out with her heel. "Before the lottery, my biggest pay increase came from the Tooth Fairy."

"Good place to start," Dick said. "Expectations."

"I went from a quarter to a dollar per tooth in one year. That's a 400 percent increase."

Dick held a notepad and pencil at the ready. He wanted to return to the therapy business so bad that he nearly salivated in anticipation of a genuine problem. "How did that make you feel?"

"Euphoric."

"As good as winning the lottery?"

Jerry shut his ears from the conversation. He studied the posters from birthing class upon the wall. The stages of delivery plodded across the yellow plaster in cartoon replication. He imagined how his child with Chelsea might have arrived. Blonde hair and blue eyes, he hoped. His thoughts danced around that place in his mind where he'd promised to never go again.

"Jerry?" Dick called. "Do you have a comment about that?"

Jerry saw the others staring. How long had he been daydreaming?

"Why don't you join the conversation?" Dick had been fighting for weeks to get Jerry involved.

Jerry frowned. Wasn't showing up enough? He laughed and nodded with the others. He made small talk. Chelsea would be proud. He'd made friends on his own, sort of, if that's what you called a ragtag group of Richie Rich's who groped for affirmation and apologizes. "What would you like me to say?"

"Arlene thinks that the money is a spiritual endowment to the truly deserving."

Jerry balked at Dick's conclusion. When did Arlene reach Zen oneness with a pile of cash? She'd been discussing the Tooth Fairy. "You think so?"

"Look at the odds." Arlene beamed. "It's amazing anyone wins."

"I guess so."

"Don't you agree? You have a better chance of getting struck by lighting."

"Does that mean we're going to be hit by lighting next?" Jerry heard a few members laugh. He hadn't meant to be funny.

"No." Arlene's brown glow sank into her styrofoam cup. She lit up another cigarette.

"I'm sorry. I think it's dumb luck."

"Fine," Dick interrupted. "Jerry's a pragmatist."

"No, I don't think I can take it to a higher plane like that. I'm not sure I was ever heading there." Jerry tried to think where he'd been heading before the lottery. All roads passed through Chelsea, so he shut that part of his brain again, even though it refused to stay closed.

Dick perked up, pencil in hand. "Jerry's just brought up an interesting point."

"What's that?" Jerry waited for Dick's next nugget of wisdom.

"We haven't examined the pre-lottery emotion. We seem to be dwelling on the after effects. Perhaps if we put them into comparison. Jerry?"

Jerry massaged the bridge of his nose with his thumb and forefinger. Dick was trying to run a can opener around Jerry's head again. Jerry wanted no part of it.

Dick scribbled on the paper. "Do you acknowledge the impact that receiving an enormous check had on your life?"

"I'm still the same person."

"Who is that?"

"Jerry Nearing. Born in Chesterfield, New Jersey."

"Really?"

"I wake up in the same bed every morning, the bed I was in before the lottery."

"Do you feel that makes you the same person?"

Jerry stopped talking. He wasn't the same. He knew that. He drifted from sunrise to sunset. He didn't work. He no longer cooked elaborate gourmet meals, opting for frozen dinners and takeout sandwiches. For the first time, he failed to live his life. He looked ahead to a time when he might restore things as they were, and every scenario involved Chelsea, at least a reasonable facsimile of her. The Chelsea in his dreams still smiled with that odd lip and strapped her arms across his chest at night. She reorganized his sock drawer on a whim. She curled up beside him after a successful meal and recounted the minutia of her day in gentle sweeping tones. He used to believe he was dreaming about better times then, when in fact he was living life to the fullest.

"Jerry?" Dick leaned forward in the chair.

Jerry glanced at the door.

"Jerry?" Dick called. "Are you with us?"

He was angry, as angry as he ever recalled in the past. The entire trip back from the JCC, Jerry cursed and muttered to himself. He tore up his driveway with the Ford, the gravel shooting from his wheels. He left the keys in the ignition and stomped inside the house.

Unsure of his target, he spun his sights around the room. His brain hummed, electric, a wonderful mind-numbing rage. He wanted to tear down a wall.

He sprinted upstairs and threw open the bedroom closet. Chelsea's abandoned shoes were scattered about the baseboards like discarded betting stubs at a horse track. He gathered them into his arms and tossed them through the window. They plunged down upon the damp evening lawn. A pair of high heels pierced the soil and stuck in the air.

Chelsea's old clothes hung in odd bunches beside his flannel shirts. He ripped them down. The wire hangers stretched and sprung like bows, shooting into the rear of the closet, recoiling toward his feet. He scooped up a shirt he'd bought for Christmas and a dress she'd found on their honeymoon, and he snatched the framed photo off the bureau. The bulk of it took flight after her shoes. He caught a glimpse of her bright white teeth in the moonlight, as the photo crash-landed and shattered in the dirt.

Jerry stood by the windowsill, shaking, sweating inappropriately for the season and time of day. His hands ached and tensed, and his head screamed for the blood of something that he couldn't quite make out. He saw the safe in the back of the closet.

The five hundred pound, fireproof, waterproof safe had a double lock and was bolted to the floor. Two months ago, Jerry installed it and filled the top shelf with fifty thousand dollars. 'Fun money,' he called it, but he wasn't having fun, so most of the cash remained inside.

He fisted the bundles of crisp bills still in their wrappers. It was the money—this very money—that had driven Chelsea mad. He hurled the bundles toward the lawn.

Outside, Jerry kicked everything into a circle. He clutched a five-gallon gas can from the shed and a book of matches.

Cortez lay beside the stump used for chopping wood. The black dog kept twenty yards shy of the action, silent, nary a whimper. He propped his snout on his front paws and watched his master. Every animal except man possesses the instinct to stand back from trouble and hold silent.

The pile ignited fast and hot. A mushroom cloud burst into the air, a carbon copy of the nuclear fusion in Jerry's head. Atoms of thought collided and merged, blowing sky high with the flames and ash. He breathed harder, sensing the heat on his face. He stayed close, compelled to experience the change erupting both inside and out.

He stared through the flames. Snippets of US currency transformed into glowing red parachutes, rising into the air. They lifted up and over the old farmhouse and the deteriorating barn. They flew over the grassy fields and blooming thickets of wild roses. The hundred year oaks drew witness, as did the ancient stars above. Everything must go: the house, the clothes, the truck, the memories of love, the smells and the tastes of it. Purge it all. It's poison. He needed to cut open a vein and bleed it free.

CHAPTER 8

FIRE SALE

J erry placed an ad in the paper, and on a chilly April morning, he kicked open the doors to the contents of his life. People roved throughout his house, hunting for bargains. He stood in the living room and listened to the footfalls of strangers. He didn't care if they stole his stuff. He wanted it out of sight. He'd decided to reshape his world from the wallet on out.

"What's the price for this?" A petite old woman bent over Jerry's coffee table. She looked down, baring her teeth like an irritated raccoon.

"Thirty bucks." Jerry guessed at what she wanted to hear. He disliked haggling.

The old lady ran her palm over the table's wood laminate edge. "There's a chip on it."

"It's used, ma'am."

"I'll give you ten."

"Fifteen, and I'll haul it to your car."

"Twelve-fifty."

"Sold." Jerry lifted the coffee table and carried it to a lemon yellow Pinto hatchback parked out front. Ten years ago, he and Chelsea brought the table home on a rainy afternoon. They sat beside it on the floor, with a fresh baguette, a wedge of Port Salut, and a bottle of Beaujolais. It was their second piece of furniture after the bed.

Jerry spotted a young couple from New Hope still lashing his bed to the roof of their car. Jerry put it out of his mind. He slid the table into the Pinto's trunk, hoping to vacate another memory.

The old lady looked pleased. Her tiny teeth chattered as she spoke. "I think I'll give the kitchen a look-see."

"Be my guest." Jerry peered down on the vicious little shopper. "Fifty bucks, and you get the contents of the lower cabinets. There's professional pans in there."

Her grandmotherly eyes lit up like a furnace door. "How much?!"

"Fifty."

"We'll see about that."

Jerry heard tires on the driveway stones. A pink Neon approached. He remembered when GM introduced the model. He loathed the trendy colors. The car appeared entirely too disposable.

Gina Spagnoli emerged from the Neon. Her trademark pink sneakers stepped outside. "Jerry?"

He let the young woman join him. She wore fancy blue jeans, a pink sweater, and her ruby necklace, not an undesirable sight in the least. He flinched, recalling that moment in the basement of Princeton Memorial Hospital.

"I see you took my advice," Gina said. "I hope you aren't leaving town."

"I'm staying at the Hyatt, until I calculate my next move." He wished he hadn't said it like that, but what did it matter? His decisions belonged to him. Whenever he conceived an idea in the past, he needed to sound it off Chelsea for approval, retooling even. Let Cogdon jump that hurdle—a tall order for a little man.

"Can I look you up?" Gina asked.

"We might cross paths." The statement felt liberating. He paused to drink in her cute fresh face. He wondered if she'd take him on now.

"Can I look around?"

"Be my guest. It's all junk to me." He wore his newfound indifference oddly. That was his problem. He over-thought things and got jammed up. He determined to let things run their course, see what happens without making any tough decisions.

Jerry headed for the barn, where Jacob Johansen had been sniffing around the farm tools since sunrise. Aged and rusting farm implements hung from the rafters, some used for a horse hitch, others for slaughtering. Jerry didn't know the names of half of them. They were in the barn when he bought the farm at an estate auction.

Jacob lingered beside the John Deere tractor. Several blades dangled from an overhead beam. If they dropped on the spot, they'd shred the octogenarian farmer like a bread slicer. "That's some collection you have here."

"They're colonial, I think."

"Could be."

"You want them?" Jerry dug his hands in his pockets, preparing to surrender the collection. He took pity on his neighbor. Farms in this neck of the woods were being gobbled up like chicken feed by tract housing.

"I'm interested." The farmer had deep wrinkles in his face, but his eyes were vibrant green like budding oak leaves. He put his hands behind his back. "How much you asking?"

"Take them."

"For real?"

"Take all of them."

"Thank you, much." Jacob scraped his boot in the dirt floor. His laces were untied, hanging beside the scored leather. "How much for everything?"

"The tractor?" Jerry didn't need a tractor either.

"The tractor, the barn, the house."

"You can't afford that."

"That's not your concern."

Gina hadn't traveled far, bugging the entire conversation from the rickety barn door. She cleared her throat, stepping between the men. "Let me handle this. Real estate is my forte."

"Gina," Jerry said, "don't bother ..."

She pressed her palm against his breastbone, backing him off like the referee in a boxing match. "Don't worry. He has the money."

"I don't ..."

"He sold a forty-acre parcel in Amwell last year to a developer. People in my business know Jacob. He owns more land around here than God."

"Good deal," Jerry said. He longed to be that kind of rich, the kind that few people knew about, but he was long past that point. Even the paperboy peered at him sideways if he didn't leave a big tip.

Gina drew intense focus on the land baron farmer, not unlike the old lady rummaging through Jerry's kitchen cabinets. "This farm is connected to your property. I assume you want to join the two."

"Yes," Jacob sighed. He seemed familiar with Gina. He looked to address his remarks to Jerry but to no avail.

Gina winked at Jerry. "I think we can reach an agreement."

"I'm offering two hundred thousand." The wrinkles in Jacobs face folded back like shutters.

"Hit the road," Gina said. "It's worth at least a half million. There's ten acres here."

Jerry stood with his arms folded. How did she know that? With the trees and broken down fences, you'd never guess where the property began and ended.

"The house is about to collapse," Jacob said. "And that carriage house up front—I'm surprised the wind hasn't knocked it down yet."

Gina glanced at the farmhouse. "Looks like everything's standing to me. It's a palace to the right family."

"Look at the roof on the main house."

"I think I'll buy this farm for myself."

"I don't want the house, but look at the condition of the clapboard, will you? It's buckling and rotten."

"If you don't want it …" Gina threw up her hands.

The lady who purchased the coffee table scampered into the barn. She appeared younger, a bounce to her step. "Mr. Nearing, what are you asking for this?"

She held a teapot that Chelsea's mother brought from England. Hand painted pictures of the British countryside—horses on a steeplechase—scrolled around the chubby sides in a Wedgwood blue color. Chelsea loved that pot. Jerry wondered why she hadn't taken it. "Where did you find it?"

"In the cabinet beside the oven."

He gazed at it. Chelsea used to curl up in the breakfast nook with a pot of tea. She looked out the window and identified the birds in the fruit trees, calling their names aloud. He'd be flipping pancakes on the griddle or carving up a grapefruit, listening to the joy in her discoveries. "Goldfinch," she'd say. "Cardinal. Humming Bird."

"It's not the nicest I've seen," the old woman said. "What's the price?"

He considered sticking the pot in a box and shipping it to Chelsea. Another man might sell it or smash it to pieces out of spite, but that wasn't his style. "It's not for sale."

"The ad said everything was for sale."

"Not that."

"I'll give you twenty dollars."

"I said it's not for sale."

"Twenty-five." She polished the pot with her sleeve, until Jerry wrenched it from her hands.

"Here's the deal," Gina interrupted in a half whisper. "I have him committed to three hundred and fifty, but he wants the truck and tractor thrown in. Will that close the deal? I can hold out for more."

"When did I say I was selling the farm?" Jerry supposed that the yard sale explained everything. He was cashing out of his old life.

"I just assumed."

"Hear me," the old woman chattered, "twenty-seven fifty. That's more than it's worth."

"No." Jerry clutched his big arm around the pot.

"Thirty. That's my final offer."

His glance darted between Gina and the old woman. They demanded answers. In his mind, he balanced his hand on the lever of a large and powerful machine. He didn't know the machine's purpose. He'd never seen it before. He wasn't even sure if he was starting it up or shutting it down, but nothing was going to be the same once he pulled the stick.

"No on the teapot." His voice echoed in his head. "And yes on the house."

The old lady huffed out of the barn. He watched her, relieved to banish her from sight. The belly of the teapot pressed against his ribs.

Jerry turned, seeing Gina shake Jacob's hand. The farm was gone. He couldn't believe it, not all at once. He'd sold the farm, severed the cord that connected him with the past. It was that easy. He felt like a newborn, just into the light, recoiling at his first glimpse of the strange new world. He wasn't breathing yet. Someone ought to slap him.

Jerry took a breath, followed by a few more. Pretty soon, breathing felt normal again. When you make big changes, you open a bottle of champagne or call someone on the phone, but he wasn't a drinker and his friends were returned to Chelsea after the annulment. He wrote her a postcard and dropped it in the mail. When Gina called to celebrate the sale of the farm, he accepted her invitation and descended from the Hyatt penthouse suite for the first time in days.

Gina chose a dark French restaurant on the main drag in Princeton. He ate lamb chops and potatoes by candlelight. Gina dined on an animal organ that he didn't recognize. He'd paused at the armory of flatware flanking his dinner plate. He hadn't employed a knife and fork in a while. He'd gotten used to eating with his fingers or at the end of a tilted cereal box.

He watched her mouth move in tiny circles as she chewed. Her toe kept riding up the cuff of his pants. She didn't talk as much as when he lay in the hospital bed. She winked at him often. She expected him to taste the wine and choose the dessert. He needed to figure out women again, although he'd never figured them out to begin with. He'd fallen in and out with Chelsea by two incredible strokes of luck. He didn't expect lightning to strike again in his lifetime.

After he paid in cash and left ten dollars with the coat check girl, Jerry found the limousine waiting by the curb. He saw Gina ducking inside. He got in behind her.

The car cruised up Nassau Street. They'd be at the hotel in minutes. He was nervous, undecided whether to invite her up or drive her home. He rationalized that he'd already had his hands on her chest all those months ago.

"I can go home with you." A knot formed in his throat. "I mean, I can ride you home."

"Either way." Gina slid beside him on the seat. Her dress was black with subtle gold flecks. You only saw it when you were up close, like when she pressed up against him.

Her leg draped over his knee, as she took hold of the knob of his shoulder with both hands. Through the slit in the side of her dress, he noticed the pink straps holding up her black stockings.

The driver rolled up the privacy screen. Shadowy hulks of trees and buildings passed by the tinted glass.

Gina's eyes were dark brown, perhaps a tad too closely set, not a big problem. He felt her breath on his face. She liked to crowd him. She'd never remind him of Chelsea, thank God.

"I'm going to make this easy for you," she said. "I like flowers and jewelry. I want to go on vacations. I don't like getting dirty. I'm twenty-six. My mother and grandmother each gave birth to five children. If you don't like my family, you don't have to speak to them. If there's something that you want in bed, you have to ask, unless of course you don't know what you like, and then we can figure it out."

He let her undo his necktie. How Gina-like. She was closing the deal on the spot. Perhaps he needed a deal-closer in his life.

She kissed him and pushed away to undo the back of her dress. Jerry kept thinking about foreplay—what he might say, where to touch her first, how fast or slow, all the complicated things meant to define sex—but here she was shedding her clothes in the limo. They weren't going to make it back to the penthouse. His pulse heightened. He wished he'd finished that glass of wine at dinner.

"Tell the driver to take it slow." She straddled his lap, bare-chested, a pink garter belt anchoring her stockings to her thighs.

He groped for the intercom. "Take us to New Brunswick, please."

"Yes, sir." The driver replied. The speaker clicked off.

Jerry heard the slight tremor in his voice. To appear cool, he needed to keep his mouth shut.

"Is this your first time since ... ?" Gina unbuttoned his shirt.

"It's been a while," he admitted. Her skin felt soft in his hands. Gina never exercised. It wasn't in her nature. He pictured her after having children—larger, stately. He'd get used it. She'd always be younger.

"It's not a problem." She ripped the belt from the loops of his pants. It cracked like a whip. "Let's take it at your pace."

He didn't love her, although he questioned the value in it. If he had to recreate the ideal woman, wouldn't it be like Gina? She was willing, flexible. She wanted to be comfortable. Was that too much to ask?

His pants and underwear bunched around his ankles and shoes. Gina unsnapped her underwear. The straps of the garter belt fell free like the ribbons on a present. Maybe Arlene was right. The good life was an endowment to the truly deserving, although he wondered what he'd done to deserve this.

He pressed her to his chest, working with her, trying to discover her style. He discovered his desire in the mix.

"That's it, baby," she said. "Touch me there."

He raised his legs, bracing them against the seat, kicking the stereo by accident. Heavy metal music blasted from the console. Gina covered her ears and screamed.

Jerry scrambled to turn down the volume in the dark. He fumbled with the little knobs, first setting the balance and tone, before clicking off the radio. "Sorry about that."

Gina's minxish expression resurfaced in the quiet. "Sorry about what?" She took Jerry down across the seat.

In minutes, he was riding the night train through the back roads of New Jersey. Gina cooed beneath him, sliding her hips down the smooth upholstery. He was king of the world again. He did as he pleased. He should have thought of this with Chelsea. She was waiting for him to raise the bar. He was going places he'd never imagined. He was going to screw the world as he pleased.

The driver hit the brakes, and he went tumbling to the floor. Gina screamed, torn from her passion with an elbow to the nose.

She clutched her face. She was bent over the hump on the floor, her limbs entangled with his. "I think I'm bleeding."

The limo pulled away from the traffic light. The green light faded to a dot.

Jerry panicked, naked, lost in disaster. He stared at the drop of blood welling in her nostril. "I'm sorry."

Gina wanted no apologies. She stuffed a wad of tissue in her nose and mounted him like a thrown horseman.

"We're going to do this right here." Her voice was nasally, but she started riding him on the floor, bracing herself against the seats. Gina swung her hips, chest bouncing with the potholes in the road. She grabbed hold of Jerry's shoulders, taking him all the way home.

Jerry let her run. He'd never view Route 27 the same way again.

The limousine navigated as if on autopilot. Gina's nose stopped bleeding. Jerry saw a thin ring of blood crusting her left nostril.

He helped her dress, slipping the black material over her freckled arms. The floral smell of sex and perspiration lingered in the back seat. Or was it Gina's rosy perfume?

She tucked the pink garter in his suit jacket. He felt it bunch against his wallet. "What's that for?"

"A memento."

"Oh." He wasn't about to dispose of it in front of her, but her perfume irritated his nose, and she was talking nonstop. He stared out the window, trying not to meet her eyes. He resisted the feeling of revulsion men get after quick and easy sex.

"The beaches in Aruba are fantastic," she said.

"I hadn't heard."

"The people want to wait on you. They want you to be happy."

Jerry watched the Mercer Oak pass by in the night. The tree stood alone in a field. It was hundreds of years old, struck by lighting and patched together by experts. The iron tie rods that bound the trunk glinted in the moonlight. "There's the oak."

"Who cares about that thing?" Gina said. "I was telling you about Aruba."

He loathed her tone of voice. "I did once."

"What are you talking about?"

"Chelsea and I used to picnic beneath it. That's all." He stopped short of saying it was their special spot. Old memories filled his palate, as he recalled the many meals they'd shared beneath the oak's sprawling branches.

"You're not still thinking about her?" She slid beside him.

He heard her switch on the charm. Her perfume crashed through his memories, turning his stomach. "Yes, I am."

"Don't you have better fish to fry?"

This analogy irked him, especially since he disliked fried fish.

She rubbed his chest. "It's me I hope."

He let her touch him. It was easier than asking her to stop. "I want the best."

"You should have the best." Her head nuzzled his shoulder.

He listened to the wheels roll beneath them. A limousine hummed like no other vehicle. Gina was right. He needed someone to share his wealth and time, but she wasn't it. No doubt about it. Gina was history. Not even iron tie rods could bind this union. He counted the minutes before they said good night.

CHAPTER 9

THREE WOMEN AND ONE GURU

"I picture you with a woman of taste and character to match your financial assets." Carmen Ruiz spoke with Jerry in the discovery room of her Mill Hill office. They sat on streamlined chairs with sloped backs and hard cushions. Video equipment waited in the corner, while Wynton Marsalis played on the stereo. Cool horns blended with Trenton's brawling daytime traffic.

Jerry took a breath, submitting himself to the interview process. He'd discovered Ms. Ruiz's matching service in the yellow pages. He noticed her accent over the phone, but in person, he thought that she dressed like a former first lady. Her short black hair shaped her head, and she wore a deep red suit with a contrasting black collar. A diamond stickpin of a heart glimmered upon her chest.

"May I call you by your first name?" She asked.

"Yes."

"Don't be embarrassed by your station, Jerry. This is the way it's been done throughout the ages. A man gathers wealth. A woman refines it."

"I never thought of it that way." He used to hand over his paycheck to Chelsea. Was that the same thing?

"May I give you some advice?" She pressed her fingertips together, like a divining rod seeking water. She aimed in his direction. "Lose the suit. It's decades past style."

His face flushed. Ruiz was forthright and determined. She'd make the tough decisions for him. He was relieved.

"The things we discuss here, never leave this office," she said. "I can arrange for you to meet a tailor. He's excellent. And perhaps a stylist too?"

"Please."

"I've put aside some profiles." She gave him a reassuring glance. "I have many clients in my repertoire, but I'm thinking of one in particular."

She handed him a thin black binder with a client number on top. "I've already spoken to her. She's interested."

Jerry placed the binder in his lap, not wanting to seem overanxious, but he differed from no other man on the planet. He hoped for a picture. That was the first thing.

"She didn't need to see a video of you," Ruiz continued, "but now that I've seen you in person, I notice that you're a tall, earthy, and robust man. You are not unattractive, which is a plus. My client won't be displeased."

"Why didn't she want to see me?"

"At this financial level, women are not necessarily interested in a man's natural appearance."

Jerry opened the binder to a glossy color photograph and a few pages of personal details.

Carmen Ruiz came alongside. "She's twenty-nine years old, the daughter of an investment banker from the Netherlands. She's been around the world."

"She likes to travel?"

"She's ready to settle down. Her name is Scarlett Hydell."

Jerry called for the valet at the Hyatt to bring his car around. At Ms. Ruiz's behest, he'd rented a Porsche 912—red with a convertible roof. He plucked his new silk sport coat off the chair and headed for the penthouse door.

Cortez rolled over on the carpet in a patch of sun. The big dog looked heavy and tired. He moaned. His dark eyes focused on nothing in particular. He missed the open space on the farm.

"See ya, old boy," Jerry said and shut the door.

The air outside the hotel was typical New Jersey summer sticky. Jerry tossed the valet five dollars and ducked into the Porsche to let the air-conditioning blast his head. He was nervous enough about his date with Scarlett. He didn't need to arrive at her doorstep with a sweaty face.

He drove to Lawrenceville and up the long drive to the Hydell estate. The house was a stone mansion set beyond view of the main road, and just beyond the barns and greenhouses, several horses gathered beneath the shade of mature ash trees. It impressed Jerry how the rich hid sprawling properties among the regular citizens. He felt as if he should be manning the old pickup truck, with the pitchfork in back and the stink of manure about his boots. A man like himself, whether dressed in designer threads or not, was a step away from hard labor and calluses. It resided in his choice of words. He'd never get the grease out from under his fingernails.

The houseman led Jerry to the garden terrace. Stone urns overflowed with geraniums and ever-blooming begonias. The country smell soothed him. He gazed over the lush lawn, which was cut into a neat grid like a football field. Two Mexicans in baseball caps shaved the far hedges into razor corners. Ms. Ruiz's mantra replayed in Jerry's head. You deserve this. You deserve this. You deserve …

Scarlett entered the terrace in a loose-fitting pants suit like pajamas yet tied with a cotton rope. She skirted the edge of the swimming pool. She possessed straight brown hair and eyes the color of old parchment. Her features appeared bleached by the sun. "Hello, Mr. Nearing."

"Pleased to meet you." Jerry searched her expression. Her thin lips formed a thoughtful line. He took her hand but didn't know what to do with it. He squeezed her fingers and released.

"You're my third match," she said.

"Ms. Ruiz didn't mention. I'm new to this. I guess I should've asked."

"That's the point which interested me the most."

"What point?"

"Your newness."

"I'm new to everything lately."

"But it's good, yes?"

Jerry had read a lot of books, especially as a boy. He enjoyed history and the old fiction classics. Some stories involved warring kingdoms and arranged marriages. They were complete fantasies. He never imagined being part of that world.

"I'm not going to bite you," Scarlett said.

He deferred to the list of questions in his head. He wasn't a great talker and prepared a conversation in advance. "I saw that you went to Vassar."

"I specialized in Medieval and Renaissance women's studies."

"What can you do with that?"

She stared at him blankly.

"Is there a job opening?" he asked again.

She returned the same empty expression. She didn't appear annoyed. It was like trying to read a brand new sleeve of paper.

He started to sweat. Perspiration burned beneath his armpits. He resisted the urge to take out a handkerchief and wipe his upper lip. "What do you do with your free time?" He figured she owned plenty of that.

"I just finished sailing around the world."

"No kidding."

"A group of us took a catamaran from Newport to San Diego, the hard way."

"Sounds hard already. Did you enjoy it?"

"We stopped along the way. Madagascar. Sydney."

"How long did it take?"

"More than a year."

He peered down on this idle waif. What was he doing last year? Shoveling horse dung, not far from her house. He understood the irony. When she set sail to conquer the globe, he was the very last man on her horizon.

"Aperitif?" she asked.

They walked to a bar cart by the pool. Jerry accepted a glass of white Burgundy and scooped up a handful of puffy crackers. He didn't want to eat or drink too much in front of her. He recalled how sick he used to be around Chelsea in the beginning. He was in love then, heart-struck as a puppy.

"I admit that I'm not much of a sailor," Jerry said.

"Can you fly?"

"If I have to."

"I fly ultra lights from time to time."

"I'm not much of a flier either. I get motion sickness."

"Is it serious?"

"I'm okay if I pop a pill."

"I'd find that a burden." Sunlight reflected off the pool, rippling across her flimsy outfit.

"I'm okay while driving," he said. "When I'm behind the wheel, I'm solid."

"That's good."

"Why's that?"

"I don't drive."

He wondered if she meant *couldn't* or *didn't* drive.

"I don't know how," she said.

He thought not to laugh. "You're kidding."

"No."

Jerry stopped talking. No doubt, he had his problems, but she seemed unprepared for the real world. What if he fell sick and needed a lift to the hospital? What if the car got a flat tire? What if someone dropped the bomb and they needed to forage for food? These were practical concerns, and he doubted she was fit to handle more than a jib sail or a dialogue on Dark Age feminism. When the chips were down, she'd fold up like a cheap chair. She'd make him soft and stupid.

"I used to own a farm in Hopewell," he said. "I used to assemble car parts in Trenton for a living. I worked with my hands."

"It's a good thing you don't have to do that anymore."

Jerry chomped on a cracker. "Those were the best years of my life."

John Coltrane buzzed in Ms. Ruiz's office. Jerry had to ask who it was. He didn't know a thing about jazz. There was a lot to learn about being sophisticated. What to leave in? What to leave out? It gave him a headache, like assembling a complicated recipe by just viewing the picture.

"Scarlett wasn't your type." Ms. Ruiz wore a green suit with a rich paisley print. "We've learned some things from that experience."

Jerry barely listened. He felt defeated. He was thirty-three years old and dead in the dating pool. He used to think that life got better every year, but he'd been cut loose and sent to pasture during his prime.

"I thought she was a good match," Ruiz said. "I'm sorry."

"It's not your fault. We're not from the same background."

"Jerry, your background has changed." She was starting to sound an awful lot like Dick Leigh. "Do you think the Vanderbilt's and Kennedy's were the heirs of nobility? They created their pedigree out of nothing, common stock even."

"I'll always be what I am. The high life isn't for me."

"Then tell me what lifestyle is?"

He didn't have an answer. When he didn't own a dime, he used to dream like a millionaire. He was no longer certain that millionaires dreamed at all.

"Do you hope to have children one day?" Ruiz asked. "You want the proper environment for them."

"I do." Jerry believed that love and an even hand was the proper way to raise kids. He guessed he was wrong about that too.

"I have another woman for you." She passed him a thin black binder. "Her name is Karen Leforte."

"She sounds familiar."

"She was an Olympic gold medalist."

"I remember. The parallel bars, right?"

"The balanced beam."

"That's it."

"She's in great shape."

He recalled an incident in Japan. He was vague on the details: police, hospitals. He wasn't the type to read the tabloids. "Didn't she have a nervous breakdown or some-thing?"

"That was years ago."

"How's she doing?"

"Fine. She's putting out a line of fitness videos."

"I'm surprised she needs a dating service."

Ruiz bristled at the remark. Her knuckles bunched, as she pressed her fingertips together and aimed them at Jerry. "She's looking for someone with similar roots."

"I don't know. What do we have in common?"

"You're both country. She grew up in Pennsylvania. Her father owns a car dealership in Newtown. She's a regular girl."

He figured that she knew how to change a flat tire at least. He pieced together his memories of her on television curling over the bars like a flexible doll, but she looked grown up in the color glossy from the binder. She was a woman.

"It's a great match," Ruiz insisted. "You've both been thrust into notoriety by circumstance."

Jerry drove to Blackfoot Lake, deep in the Jersey Pine Barrens. The evergreen scent in August was bold and crisp, and the lake was active with weekend boaters. On the oppo-site shore, the annual skeet shooting contest commenced. A slight breeze swept through the open space, and the reports of gunfire and cheers riffled across the muddy waters.

The pier was abandoned by late morning. Empty boat trailers jammed the parking lot, and colorful windsurfers and canoes dotted the lake. Jerry scanned the docks for Karen Leforte. He recognized her right away. She sat beside a bearded man in a bright orange turban.

Karen Leforte wore a navy blue tracksuit with white racing stripes down the arms and legs. Jerry agreed with Ms. Ruiz. Karen was in great shape. She looked effervescent and attractive, probably the same age as he was. His hands tingled with excitement.

He approached her, dressed in a designer polo shirt, chinos, and flat brown deck shoes. The man with the turban sat too close to Karen. As the first order of business, Jerry planned to invite her on a stroll around the lake, but he noticed the pair speaking closely.

"This is Rashied." Karen nudged her head toward her companion. She didn't offer further explanation.

Rashied smiled. His beard was black like the eyebrows that nearly bridged his nose. He wore a three-piece suit with an orange tie that matched his turban.

Jerry wondered if Rashied spoke English. He decided to ignore him and direct his request at Karen only. "Would you like to walk the lake?"

"This is our first outing," Karen said. "Let's sit and talk."

Jerry enjoyed the sound of her voice. It was energetic but not intrusive. He realized that he'd never heard it before, only viewed her in magazines and on television. He took a seat on the opposite side from Rashied. Several shotgun blasts echoed across the lake, followed by more cheers.

"Did you have trouble finding the lake?" Karen asked.

"It's on the map."

"Ms. Ruiz filled me in about you."

"I read your report too."

"My report?"

"She profiles prospective matches."

"Oh, right."

Rashied leaned over and whispered in Karen's ear. She stared at the horizon, listening intently. Jerry failed to make out a word.

"Do you two have business to take care of?" Jerry asked. "I can leave you alone for a while."

"Please, sit."

"I just thought ..."

"You thought what?"

He watched Rashied whisper again. He tried not to get annoyed. "What is he doing?"

Karen returned her focus to Jerry. She showed some of that girlish expression that Jerry recalled from the past, as if a panel of judges were about to flip scorecards and grade the entire exchange. "Rashied's a trusted advisor."

"Like, on the spot?" Jerry believed he was making a joke.

"Yes."

"Oh."

"Do you mind?"

"No. It's alright. No, no. It's no problem." He listened to himself say 'no' too many times.

"I'm glad you understand."

"Does he go everywhere with you?"

Rashied whispered again.

"Did I ask the wrong question?" Jerry asked.

"Excuse me?"

"Is there something Rashied wants to ask me?"

Rashied pulled away from her ear. He smiled at Jerry.

Oh brother. Jerry felt the bottom quickly dropping out of this arrangement. Life offered a number of trap doors, and there were times when he wanted to fall through one.

He folded his hands in his lap. He recalled his silly list of questions. Experience had pared it down to the basics. "Do you know how to drive a car?"

She glanced at Rashied. "Yes, I can drive."

"Good." His glanced darted between her and her advisor. "Can either of you change a flat tire?"

"Excuse me?"

"Can you change a flat tire?"

She and Rashied both stared.

"How about this one," Jerry said. "If the bomb dropped tomorrow, what would you do?"

"I don't understand." Karen glanced at Rashied.

"Does Rashied have an answer for that?" Jerry asked. "Either one of you can answer."

"Another bust." Jerry spoke into his cell phone, as he sped away from the odd twosome. The Porsche's mighty engine roared over the blacktop, as if preparing to take flight. Pine trees and patches of sand raced through his peripheral vision. He wanted to create fast miles between himself and Blackfoot Lake.

Ruiz sounded cautious over the phone. "I'm disappointed."

"I don't think she's interested in a one-on-one yet."

"Did she bring the guru?" Ruiz sounded disturbed.

"Yup."

"She didn't."

"It's okay." He found himself consoling Ruiz again. This whole experiment wasn't turning out as he hoped. "There will be others, I guess."

"Don't be discouraged, Jerry. I have a file cabinet full of women who'd be proud to know a man of your caliber."

He was afraid of that. He looked down the road as if holding a specific destination in mind, but plenty of time remained before the Saturday night buffet at the Hyatt. The big decision was whether to turn left or right at the next intersection. "I'm sure you're hard at work."

"I can profile a few candidates for you over the phone." She shifted files in the background. Charlie Parker bopped through the receiver. He was beginning to recognize the jazz masters from his compilation CD.

"That won't be necessary." He saw steam rising from the hood of a blue Datsun on the side of the road. Its flashers were going. He signaled to pull over. "I'll call you in a few days."

"Don't wait."

"I won't."

"You need to stay in circulation. Every date makes you more desirable."

"We'll talk on Monday." He squeezed the power button on the cell phone and stopped several yards ahead of the troubled car.

Jerry rose out of the Porsche, in his spiffy designer clothes. The sun beat down, and the air smelled like anti-freeze and hot grease. Cars whipped past on the open road. The breeze barely fanned the midday heat.

A woman leaned against the door, arms folded. She was dressed in trim black pants and a white buttoned-down shirt. Jerry saw relief in her expression. She pushed off her car, joining him halfway on the shoulder.

"Thank you." She was a blonde, with lanky arms like his former wife. Her tan skin reflected the color of burning wood before it catches the flame.

"How long have you been out here?"

"Fifteen, twenty minutes. I stopped trying to wave down cars."

"No one stopped?"

"No one stops anymore. I'm late for work."

He gripped the cell phone in his palm. "Need to make a call?"

"Yes, please."

He turned it on and handed it over.

Jerry walked to the Datsun and leaned over the hood. The blue fog started to dissipate, although the engine still hissed. A long and ragged slit opened the lower radiator hose. Not even duct tape would help at this point, and he doubted she carried enough water and antifreeze to refill the reservoir.

The woman spoke quickly into the phone. Her job had something to do with food service. She was late for a catered affair. Jerry liked the way she took control of the conversation. She wasn't about to be blamed for a blown radiator hose.

He waited for her to hang up. "Everything alright?"

"I think so. I don't know why I take these jobs."

"For the money," he said without thinking.

She paused. She seemed to be taking in his clothes and car. "That's the reason."

"I remember those days." He recalled that women noticed details like shoes, pants, and hairstyle. Men noticed hips, chests, and hair. He wanted to say that this image wasn't really him. "It wasn't that long ago when I needed every paycheck."

"Sure. What are you, a stockbroker? No, don't tell me. You're a lawyer."

"Do I look like a lawyer?"

"You're a doctor then?"

"I took a CPR course once."

She started to laugh. It was a deep expression, laced with sincerity. She brushed back her bangs and looked him right in the eye. It was a sign. He'd read the book on female body language, which Ruiz insisted he'd study as part of his training, but he summarized the entire text as a load of bunk, until this moment.

"Do you need a lift?" He treaded slowly with his questions, trying to act casual. If he got her into his car, he'd muster the courage to ask her on a date. *Things happen this way. They must. It's just that easy.*

"Did I mention that I'm a tennis instructor in real life?"

"This must be my day for athletes."

"Why's that?" Her finger curled in her hair, another winning indication.

"By chance, I just ran into Karen Leforte."

"The gymnast?"

Good deal. He couldn't believe it. Suddenly, he was smooth, and he didn't even know her name. "I'll give you a lift and tell you about her."

"That would be great."

He swallowed his excitement. *Stay cool.*

She walked with him to board the Porsche but stopped and caught his eye. "By the way, my name is Meg O'Brien."

A week later, Jerry strolled the aisles of a new super-sized market outside of Princeton. He poked the Brie cheese with his index finger and squeezed the French bread. He sampled the roasted peppers and liver pate, searching for the right flavors to compliment lunch. The main course—prepared to Jerry's specifications by the Hyatt chef—waited in a wicker basket in the car. Meg O'Brien expected a simple picnic lunch, and Jerry planned to dazzle her.

When the automatic doors to the store parted, Cortez stood up and greeted his master. Jerry watched the big animal twitch his ears in the sun. The dog was tied to a No Parking sign by the curb. The leash was just for show. He'd wait all day without disturbing the smallest child. He was the best damned dog Jerry ever owned.

"How ya doin' old boy?" Jerry scratched Cortez behind the ears. The dog rubbed its snout against his thigh. He reached into the shopping bag and tore open a half-pound package of ground chuck.

Cortez gobbled down the bloody treat on the sidewalk, licking his chops with his long wet tongue. Overdressed Princeton housewives pushed past with carts full of groceries, sneering at the carnivorous display. The kids didn't seem to mind, and Jerry returned their happy grins. Why did adults forget what made them happy as kids? He was as guilty of this crime as the next person, but regardless, his style wasn't going to be cramped. He had a lunch date with an attractive woman, and Ms. Ruiz had nothing to do with it.

When Jerry reached Battlefield Park, he spotted Meg O'Brien seated by the monument across the lawn. Tall white columns of stone rose at her back. He pulled the Porsche to the roadside and released the dog.

"Hello." Meg shouted, waving a hand above her head. She wore a short green cotton dress and white leather sandals. Her hair was tied into a ponytail, and a stray blonde lock spiraled down in front of one eye.

Jerry noticed her tan legs. She was fit, healthy, and perhaps a tad furtive in the way she bunched her mouth to nearly a smirk, but as soon as she spotted Cortez dropping from the car, she came forward and took the dog's head in both hands.

"He's beautiful." She stroked the fur along his jowls. Some of it was turning gray.

Jerry watched Cortez lick the salt from her bare knee. He gently grabbed a fistful of fur at his hindquarter. "That's enough, boy."

"I don't mind." She let Cortez lick her face once and then stood up. "Is he a shepherd?"

"As far as I know. I rescued him from the A.S.P.C.A."

Her mouth crumpled in the corner. It was cute. "You're a rescuer, eh?"

Jerry had to think about that. He'd forgotten about stopping to assist her at the roadside. It was his custom to do so. He didn't fear strangers. He just preferred not to speak with them unless they needed help. Chelsea used to warn him against both his isolation and bravado.

"What do you call him?" she asked.

"Cortez."

"That's a powerful name."

"I used to read a lot of history." He still did, when he had the head for it. It was one way to kill time. It was either that or cooking, but the tiny kitchen in his penthouse suite didn't inspire many gourmet meals, and he never realized how much he appreciated the approval of a companion until he dined alone.

"So what's the history of Jerry Nearing?"

Jerry looked at the pretty lady. They'd chatted by phone during the week. He'd kept it light, making jokes about his career. Once he said he was a butler to a millionaire. Another time he said he'd struck oil on his farm in Hopewell. She laughed, but he knew he'd be faced with the truth eventually.

"I won the lottery," he said.

She took it like before. "No, really."

"I won the lottery."

"Are you serious?"

He saw the surprised look on her face, like he somehow didn't deserve it. 'No one does,' he wanted to say, but he didn't hold it against her. It's impossible to envision the other side. "You want some of it?"

"Sure." She grabbed hold of the little pocket near her waist. "Stuff it right in here."

"I'll have to remember that later." He couldn't believe he'd said that. He felt uncomfortable, until he realized that he'd made her blush. Being rich wasn't so bad after all.

Jerry set down the lunch basket and threw open the blanket. Across the road, he glimpsed the Mercer Oak where he and Chelsea used to picnic as middle class paupers. A memory or two passed through him like a brief and quiet wind. He didn't waste time lingering there. "Is this spot fine for lunch?"

"Yes, fine."

They began with cheese and crackers. Jerry poured Merlot into paper cups to avoid the ire of the police. He pulled the china and napkins from the basket. The chef had prepared clams on the half shell, light-battered fried chicken, slices of smoked ham, pasta salad with vegetables, and watercress salad with blue cheese and walnuts.

Meg tasted everything, devouring a plate of pasta, chicken, and clams. She wasn't shy. She sat with her legs tucked beneath her. After a second glass of wine, she laughed louder, and her sense of humor grew more sarcastic. Jerry liked it. He liked it a lot.

"Let me get that." She reached with a linen napkin and cleared a spot of raspberry pie from the edge of his lip.

"Thank you," he said.

"If I ever have something on my lip, I want you to tell me."

"No problem."

"I can't stand it when people let it sit like a zit on the tip of your nose."

"They're trying to be polite."

"Hogwash. They want you to look stupid."

"I can do that without the raspberries on my face."

"Not you."

He heard the quickness of her response. He was a different man around her. He was sailing gratefully into unknown territory.

"What are you going to do now, Jerry Nearing?" She slid a blood red piece of pie into her mouth. The sun shone off her face. He believed that he saw himself in her reflection.

"I haven't decided yet."

"Will you start a business?"

"I had the farm, but that's gone. I guess I'm looking for a new direction."

"People would love to be in your shoes."

He'd heard that remark so many times that he wanted to print up reply cards like: 'no you don't' or 'maybe you do.'

He glanced about the lawn, thinking of a new direction to spin the conversation.

Cortez was leaving, galloping across the grass.

Jerry stood up. "Cortez!"

Meg cupped her hands above her eyes to block the sun. "Where's he going?"

"It's not like him to run off." He watched the dog head for the trees. Since leaving Hopewell, Cortez visited few wooded areas. Even this sparse version had to be enticing.

"Cortez!" Jerry shouted.

"Coooorteeeez," Meg called.

"I better get him, before he's gone until sundown."

Jerry stepped after the dog. Cortez's black frame folded into the lush underbrush. Jerry saw a narrow opening in the woods and sprinted for it.

He entered the tall hardwoods, eyes adjusting to the shade. Several squirrels scattered up the trees, and dozens of sparrows took flight. He felt mosquitoes feasting on his bare calves and slapped at the bugs.

A footpath sliced through the trees. Cortez raced up the path and into daylight. Jerry pursued. A pair of joggers poured onto the path, and he shouldered past and reentered the lawn.

The edge of the woods fanned to the left and right. Cortez wasn't in sight. Jerry chose the left, gambling that Meg spotted the dog coming from the other direction.

He ran at top speed. He once owned a mastiff that grew senile and had to be put down. It was too soon for Cortez, yet perhaps a summer of hotel living had debased the dog's psyche or, even worse, compromised its loyalty.

The traffic raced past on Saturday afternoon. Jerry kept glancing at the road, fearing Cortez broke in that direction, but he failed to spot him. He ran to the end of the park before heading back.

He paced himself around the woods, catching his breath before returning to the picnic site. He still clutched the linen napkin in his hands and mopped his face.

Cortez stood with Meg at the blanket. Another blonde woman in white jogging shorts spoke with her, bending over to pat the dog's head. It took Jerry a few more steps to realize who she was. He stopped moving. His deck shoes planted in the grass. *Damn, it's Chelsea.* Cortez must have picked up her scent and ran after her. The dog often accompanied Chelsea on her morning jog.

A group of kids tossed a frisbee, laughing and screaming in the background. Jerry considered keeping his distance from Meg until Chelsea disappeared. He felt strange seeing the women together, like he was cheating on Chelsea and had been discovered, even after everything that went down between them. He decided to pick up his pace instead. He didn't know women very well, but he knew he didn't want them comparing notes.

Meg eyed him first. "There he is."

Chelsea turned around. She wore a powder blue tank top that picked up her eyes. Perspiration dampened the elastic ban above her chest. He saw the wetness in the pit of her neck. Hundreds of times she'd sauntered in from a morning jog and slid beneath the sheets to make love before work. She smelled that way now. It was a powerful elixir. "Hello, Jerry."

"Hello." His mouth felt dry.

"Cortez joined up with me on the trail."

Jerry wondered how much Chelsea told Meg. Women liked to stake claims that way, and Chelsea was exceptional at it. He typically fell blind to a come-on from another women, yet Chelsea shut it down as soon as she caught wind of it. She once 'accidentally' dumped a can of cola down the blouse of a woman who'd gotten a tad too fresh at the hospital picnic.

"He likes to run." He conjured an amiable expression, sending it in Meg's direction.

"I was talking to your date." Chelsea glanced at the spent dishes and arrangement of food on the blanket. Her eyes rose to Jerry. "It's good to see you out and mingling."

He felt ridiculous. He might have taken Meg to one hundred other places. Why here? He knew what Chelsea was thinking: another blonde, same spot, good wine and food—oh Jerry, how sweet, you still love me. He found the tone of her voice patronizing and accepted it like a mouthful of spoiled cheese.

"I'm moving on," he said, a tinge of spite in his voice. He wished she'd vanish. He'd spent months awaiting her return, and now he wanted her to leave the state. No, the country.

"You look good."

He noticed she hadn't modified her looks any further since the divorce. He expected she'd have gone under the knife for something else. "You haven't changed a bit."

Her lip drew a slight wrinkle, not that anyone noticed but him. The surgeon didn't hide everything. She wasn't entirely flawless. He watched her curl a finger by instinct, but she kept it at her side.

"Are you living in town?" he asked.

"I like the trails here," she said, as if he didn't already know.

He noticed Meg in the corner of his eye. What was she thinking? She probably didn't know what to make of this.

"Thanks for bringing the dog back," he said.

Chelsea patted the dog's fur again. "He's getting heavy."

"I'm solving that problem."

"Good deal." She dropped his old phrase, offering her hand like a stranger. "I'll be seeing you."

"Maybe." He stared at her long fingers—fingers that he no longer called his own, and then he sobered up and shook them. Her hand felt tense. It trembled slightly, totally unlike her.

He let her walk away, careful not to watch. He counted the seconds, estimating the time it took for her to reach the road. Soon the coast would be clear.

Meg watched Chelsea. "She's gorgeous. How long have you known each other?"

"A few years."

"Old girlfriend?"

He understood that she was fishing for information. "Something like that."

"Long time?"

He decided to drop the bomb. It was better to pretend like it didn't matter. Damn, of all the dumb things to have happen. "She's my ex-wife."

"She didn't say."

He glanced back to see her sneakers trailing away. The growing distance calmed him. "That's the new Chelsea."

CHAPTER 10

THIS OLD, BROKEN-DOWN, GODFORSAKEN HOUSE

J erry ambled through the penthouse for days, stopping at the huge windows overlooking Route One. New office parks and townhouses blanketed the country-side, like swarms of termites burrowing through the trees. Cortez lay in the sunny spot on the carpet. Meg's phone calls languished on the answering machine. In his dreams, he made love to a gorgeous blonde, not Meg O'Brien but his old standby, Chelsea.

Their last encounter in the park replayed in his mind. Was he fooling himself? Chelsea was a cool customer, rarely driven to a display of nerves, but she shuddered as they touched. Only Jerry noticed. It reminded him of the first time they made love.

It was the night before Chelsea departed for college. He'd kissed her odd lip, nibbled it even. He adored every part of her and wanted her to know, but his words vanished, as he fumbled with her clothes. Cotton sleeves and bluejeans slid shyly from her arms and legs. He and Chelsea had come this close before, and later they'd find confidence in lovemaking, but at that moment in Jerry's bedroom, with the cicadas singing beyond the screened windows, Chelsea flinched, as he entered her for the first time. He paused and detailed her lip with an index finger, aware that his weight above her was large. Strange scents hung in the air: smoldering ash, cut lemon. The blue glow of the lava lamp colored her face, unveiling her fear and desire. He wrapped his heart around his hopes. It was heaven, yet too brief to hold. He thought that she might never return.

For a time, Jerry clung to the mood of that night. He smelled it in the woods outside his father's house. He searched for bits of it in Chelsea's letters and quick phone calls from her dormitory. He decided to build a nest for Chelsea. He worked blind. It was a place that she mentioned but only she saw in her head. He took extra shifts at GM, gathering cash for a farm in Hopewell. He wasn't certain if Chelsea wanted to join him, yet at graduation, she suggested that they marry. It took him by surprise. It was her single greatest gesture toward him.

Below the Hyatt penthouse, a large crane balanced an iron beam in the air. Jerry watched the men lower it into position and thread the rivets. He knew what he needed to do. His life was emerging from another test of time. Once again, Chelsea was back at school. She wanted to better herself, refine her own brand of perfection. He needed a reason for her to return home.

"Six hundred thousand," Jacob Johansen announced, before crashing his sledgehammer into a steel wedge. The collision released a tiny spark.

Jerry watched the aged cut of hickory separate into two splintery hunks. The sun crested over West Amwell beyond Jacob's farm, and the day's heat abandoned the hills. Jerry noticed the birds and squirrels rustling at twilight. The impending fall wrought nervous energy from the woods. He missed the change of seasons. A return to the countryside was the right move.

"That's almost twice what you bought it for," Jerry said.

"Ain't my problem." Jacob balanced the next hickory cut upon the stump and tapped the wedge to set.

"Be reasonable, Jake. I sold the property to you as a favor."

"You were in a hurry to sell. You're in hurry to buy. Hurry has its price."

"Four Hundred. That should satisfy you."

Jacob eyed the Porsche parked along the lawn. "That's a fine ride there. How much that cost you?"

"I leased it."

"Hmmm." He tugged his gray beard and drove the heavy sledge home. The chickens cackled, protesting each swing of the hammer.

Jerry spread his arms. He knew the money game. He'd learned a lot from one summer in the penthouse. Some people wanted every dollar they clutched in their hot little hands. Only money stood between him and his ten acres of heaven in Hopewell. "What do you want from me?"

Jacob propped his wrists upon the butt end of the axe. "Seeing as we were neighbors, I'll take five hundred."

"Agreed." Jerry took Jacob's old paw in his grasp. He gave it a mighty squeeze, letting the farmer know what he thought about the deal. They wouldn't be speaking for a while.

"I can set you up with her for Thursday night." Ms. Ruiz pushed another client over Jerry's cell phone. She had a product to sell: nubile young women who were hunting for Daddy Big Bucks.

"I don't know about my schedule." Jerry pressed the receiver tight, blocking out the noise of circular saws and hammers. He watched three men pry rotten cedar clapboards from the side of the farmhouse. The smell of sawdust and moldy wood tingled his nose. A second crew tore up planks from the hardwood floor, and a priceless pile of lumber amassed in the scrap heap on the lawn.

"Are you too busy for love?" Ms. Ruiz said.

"It's not that." He didn't know how to say it. He rejected her brand of love. He stepped aside to let the video crew move past. A black cable uncoiled near his foot, tailing the man with the lights. "I'm in over my head at the house."

"I bet you're busy," Ms. Ruiz said. "I saw the first episode on television last week. I'd kill for a kitchen like that."

"At the moment, it lives only on blueprints."

"I can't wait to see it finished."

"Me too." Jerry wanted the cameras off his property, but the architect had lined up the Home Makers Show for the entire renovation. The relentless exposure grated on Jerry's nerves. He'd never agree to this arrangement, if he didn't believe Chelsea was watching their dream house come alive in weekly installments. That was the payoff. Home Makers used to be a favorite of hers, and news of it in town had reached all the papers.

"Excuse me." The show's producer tapped Jerry from behind. Mang Mun Mar's height fell shy of Jerry's shoulder. He had a slight frame and wide elusive features. Frost blanketed the fields, although Mang dressed in sweaters and collared shirts for every climate. "We need to talk."

Jerry pulled away from the phone. A month earlier, he expected the show host Shane Edlow or Babs the master carpenter to run the job, but he learned from the first day that Mang actually rebuilt the houses. Shane and Babs mugged for the cameras, sinking an occasional nail for the money shot.

"I've got to go." Jerry disconnected before Ruiz launched into her next pitch. No doubt, it was another exact match, complete in every aspect except love and chemistry.

"Bad news." Mang peered up through oval wire glasses. His expression was buttoned-down like his collar. "The foundation is antique."

"You mean, colonial."

"No, antique."

"Antique is good, isn't it?"

"For furniture."

"What do we need to do?"

"Replace it, or you're going to have big problems, very big."

"So?"

"The floors will sag. The walls will crack. Disaster."

"Can't we fix it?"

"It's going to put you over budget?"

"I don't care about the budget. That was for television."

The producer nodded and walked toward the production trailers.

Jerry thought he caught Mang showing a modicum of pleasure, but he couldn't be certain. "Quote me a price first."

Mang turned and nodded.

Jerry heard a vehicle approaching. A monster green and white pickup motored toward the house. The lid of the tool bin flapped open and closed on the bumpy road. By the way the tires tore up the grass and the tail of the truck skittered left and right, Jerry realized that Babs was in a jolly mood—which was a shame for only ten in the morning.

The truck locked its brakes, and a heavyset woman with short bleached-blonde hair dropped out of the cab. She wore bluejeans, a denim shirt, and a suede vest with Indian embroidery. A crushed green Heinekens can tumbled to the ground by her boots. "Where's my fucking table saw?"

Mang Mun Mar sent people running after her. An intern scooped the empty beer can into the truck, while another tailed Babs and buffered her from the contractors.

"Where's my shit?" Babs swallowed a belch, taking Mang in her sights. "Hey M&M, where's my setup? I told you to be ready."

If Mang revealed any expression, it was a deliberate effort to disguise his distaste for Home Maker's master carpenter. It resembled a wall against a raging sea. "In the barn," Mang said.

"Is that shit shed going to stand?"

Mang paused, perhaps considering the benefits of an untimely collapse. "The men shored it up yesterday."

"Geez, M&M, you're a regular sweetheart." She strutted toward the barn with a cordless router in one hand and a six-pack-sized cooler in the other. She paused and glanced at the man next to Mang. "Hey, Eddie."

Shane Edlow stood beside Mang. "She better not call me that on camera."

"Don't worry," Mang said.

"I'm worried." A makeup bib dangled from Edlow's neck, as a woman finished powdering his cheeks. He was a handsome man, with boxy features that complimented his beard. He stood an inch taller than Mang, and from Jerry's position, the bald spot atop his head resembled a map of Spruce Run Lake. "Is she going to be camera-ready?"

"Look at the bright side," Mang said. "We won't have to add color to her face."

"I hate when she does this. Somebody better make sure she's standing for the walk-through. I'm not waiting around for her to sleep it off."

"She'll be good, I think. We'll tape both of you, after her sidebar."

"You better. She's a beer shy of nighty-night."

Jerry sensed the cameras about to roll and planned his escape. He was halfway to his Porsche before the interns intercepted him.

Mang was hot on their heels. "You're going to stay, yes?"

"I have an appointment in town." He began fabricating excuses, fumbling through his pockets for his car keys.

"We need the homeowner on film."

"Is that really necessary? It's about the house."

"People need to put a face with the dwelling. It humanizes things."

"How about Babs? She seems pretty human."

Mang pretended he hadn't heard that. "It's in the contract. We get at least three appearances from the homeowner."

"You'll get them."

"The last time I counted, you were three short."

Jerry sucked in his stomach and stuffed his keys in his pocket. This was the new Jerry, he reminded himself. This was exactly what he wanted. Chelsea was watching the show. He knew her. She couldn't resist. The engaging face of Jerry Nearing put the finishing touches on the ultimate house.

An intern unfolded a chair for Jerry beneath a temporary canopy, and the makeup artist descended upon his face, powdering, lining, and smearing sticky gels across his cheeks and forehead. Jerry thought about his life in the briefest of sketches. To retrieve the love of his life, he must project the very opposite of what she'd once loved.

When Jerry reached the house, Shane Edlow stood in the new kitchen space. The roof and walls were knocked out, and the primary builder was overseeing construction of the extended floor plan. Work turned in insidious cycles, as scruffy carpenters performed redundant functions. It all served as a good backdrop for filming.

"So this will be the kitchen," Edlow announced in an authoritative voice. "It's a chef's delight."

The camera lights blared in Jerry's face. He stood completely still and upright, like one of the bare studs in the wall. He waited for Edlow to continue.

"Cut," Mang yelled. "Jerry?"

"What?"

"You're supposed to act as if you'd just walked into your new dream kitchen under construction."

"I have."

"Keep the flow. When Shane speaks to you, have something to say."

"Yes," Jerry said.

"Just go with the conversation. We've discussed your kitchen a dozen times. You know what to say."

"Got it."

"And please, take your hands out of your pockets."

"Got it."

"Cue the cameras, and roll."

Edlow launched into his TV voice again. "So Jerry, what do you think of your new kitchen?"

"Well, it's big." Jerry saw Mang nod beside the key grip.

"It's going to be the jewel of your new home."

"It's a mess right now."

"That's because we don't have the walls finished yet, or a roof for that matter." Edlow glanced up, and his voice suddenly dropped out of character. "Wait a minute."

Mang stopped the cameras.

"What is that?" Edlow grimaced, pointing up to second floor roof.

"It's just a camera," Mang said.

"I know what it is." Edlow nervously brushed a hand over his bald spot.

"I want brief overheads to cut in the mix."

"No, no, none of that. No overheads."

"Shane."

"I'm serious."

Mang's shoulders dropped. He glanced to his assistant. "Break it down."

One of the interns burst onto the set. She nearly tripped over a carton of nails in the foyer. "We've got an emergency."

"What is it now?" Mang sighed.

"There's been an accident in the barn."

"Did someone break something?"

The intern looked frazzled. "Babs cut off her finger."

Edlow tossed his hands in the air. "Not again!"

Everyone glanced at the show's host.

"She did this in San Francisco four years ago. I warned you, Mang."

Mang sighed again.

The crew funneled through the main hall and onto the lawn like a crowd exiting a movie theatre, but the real show lay ahead. Babs sat on her truck tailgate. A blood-soaked rag wrapped her left hand, and she fisted a can of Heineken in the other. The interns fussed over her. They wiped her head with a towel and brushed the hair from her eyes.

"I'm sorry, M&M." Babs cried while sipping beer. Foam dribbled down her cheek. "I'm so sorry."

Jerry lagged in the back, peering over everyone's head. An open cooler sat beside Babs on the tailgate. He swore that he saw a loose finger zippered inside a plastic baggie on ice.

"I'm bleeding like a motherfucker," Babs said. "Fucking table saw."

Mang looked pale. Edlow headed for his trailer to lie down. No one uttered a word.

"Where's the hospital around here?" Mang asked.

"I'll take her." Jerry moved through the crowd. He didn't have to push. People normally stepped aside for him.

He reached Babs and extended a hand to help her up. He prayed she didn't offer the one with the bloody rag. "Come with me."

"Thanks, sweetheart." She got to her feet, glancing at him like they'd never met. "Want a brewski?"

For the holidays, the Winners Circle met in the backroom of a tavern by the West Trenton railway station. Jerry assumed the corner seat and studied the party. Green and gold tinsel decorated the walls, intertwined with white blinking lights. He saw Arlene sneaking a smoke by the fire exit. She wore a mink stole and a dyed mink Santa hat. Tom lingered near the appetizer spread, scarfing puff pastries by the handful. Dick mingled with the two dozen guests, clasping hands and touching base. Jerry awaited the moment when Dick reached him.

"Merry Christmas." Dick sat beside Jerry with a plate of celery and carrot sticks and a glass of champagne. He wore a camelhair jacket and black alligator loafers.

"Tom looks good," Jerry said. "Has he lost a little weight?"

Dick glanced back. "Not for long."

"The holidays can be a killer."

"How's the house coming?"

"Good." Jerry just assumed Dick saw it on TV like everyone else and was making small talk. "The floors should be finished by the end of January, and then I need to find furniture."

"Are you hiring a decorator?"

"Only the best."

"It's an awesome project."

"I can see the light at the end of the tunnel. On Saturday, they're showing the roof episode."

"I'm surprised you went through that much trouble."

"I know. I could have built a new house for less money."

"That's part of it."

Jerry was used to Dick's probes. "What else?"

"I was wondering why you chose that house."

"You mean my old house."

"The one you and Chelsea used to share. If it were me, I'd find a new place. No memories."

Jerry fidgeted with his cocktail napkin, folding it in one hand as if performing blind origami. "I like the land."

"That much? Yesterday, I saw a lovely plot in Hopewell atop a hill. Twenty acres, I think it was."

"Sounds nice."

"I would have started fresh."

"That's you." Jerry grew warm beneath his cashmere collar.

"If it were me, I'd move out."

"I get your point."

Dick drained his champagne, eyeing Jerry past the stem of the glass. "You've been missing meetings."

"The house takes a lot of energy." In truth, Jerry felt useless during the restoration process, and countless times, he'd swapped his good shoes for a pair of work boots and started swinging a hammer or carrying sheetrock.

"You're busy at night?"

"I didn't sign up for anything when I joined the Circle."

"No, but ..."

"You better come out and say what's on your mind."

Dick's focus was searing. "What's this house really about?"

Jerry wanted to slap Dick for bringing this up at the party. "It's about making a dream come true. You know about dreams."

"Is it your dream or Chelsea's?"

Jerry didn't answer. Dick was only trying to help, but damn him. Jerry scanned the room. No one probably noticed how red he was getting.

"Jerry?"

Jerry rose from the table. He walked halfway across the room, considering a glass of wine or beer, but he saw the separation in the room divider and instinctively stepped through it. A minute later, he was driving back to his penthouse at the Hyatt.

By February, construction on the farmhouse stopped, and Jerry joined the final walk-through with Mang and Edlow. Babs was back from her morning physical therapy appointment, barking orders at the carpet installers in the bedrooms upstairs. Her first weeks in AA were rough, and everyone cut a wide berth around her.

"I remember Babs on the San Fran shoot." Edlow walked into the remodeled kitchen. An island with a sink and European propane burners dominated the southern half of the room. A bank of circumnavigating windows offered stunning views of Jacob's farm and the Sourland Mountains. "She was three weeks dry with a hard-on. Interns dropped off the set like lemmings."

A loud thump shook the ceiling. Mang bristled every time Babs stomped her boots.

Jerry ignored it. He had the farmhouse within his grasp. It was Chelsea's vision brought to fruition. Who cares what anyone else thought or did? Babs could drive ten-penny nails through the soles of his feet, and he wouldn't care.

"Let's cue the lights and start filming," Mang said, "before Babs brings the house down."

"I'm ready." Jerry saw the final show taping as their ticket off his farm. The sound of birds and trees waited to assume the absence of buzzing saws and roaring equipment generators.

"Accidents aside," Mang said, "it's been a pleasure working with you."

Jerry was taken aback. He hadn't received a genuine compliment in ages. He searched Mang's hard-to-read face. "Thank you."

"You have an eye for detail. You know what you want."

Jerry tucked the comment away in his mind. *Good deal.* Had he changed that much? He always knew what he wanted, but it was Chelsea who precipitated his ideas into reality.

Mang signaled the key grip, and the cameras began rolling.

"Shane Edlow here. Today on Home Makers, we wrap up the Nearing farm, and it's a beauty."

"Cut," Mang said. "Let's begin in this room and move out through the living room."

A dark-haired woman in a pink dress wove through the production crew from the back of the room. She caught Jerry's eye, but so many months had passed that he almost forgot who she was.

"Gina?" Jerry said.

"Hello, Jerry." Gina Spagnoli looked different. Her cheeks appeared fuller, and her voice was lower and less assertive. "Your house is wonderful."

"What are you doing here?"

"We need to talk." She waddled from behind the kneeling soundman. Her body sloped backward, and her dress bulged at the waist. That extra part of her middle seemed to be directing her forward.

"What happened to you?"

She looked down and pressed both hands gently against her waist, outlining the roundness of her belly. Her eyes rolled up with a surreptitious glance. "I'm pregnant."

Mang heard the last part of the conversation and scooted around the island. "Is this your girlfriend?"

Jerry didn't answer. He calculated quick numbers. How long was it? Seven months? Eight? Oh God, Gina looked ready to pop.

"Why didn't you mention her?" Mang's face assumed more expression than ever before. It nearly twisted into a question mark.

Jerry's mouth moved. "I didn't think ..."

"This is super. Let's get her in the shot." Mang sent the crew into a new flurry of activity.

"We can't ..." Jerry's voice was shaky. His arms and legs felt as if he'd soaked them in ice water.

"Why not?"

"Yes," Gina bubbled. "Why not?"

Jerry considered a dozen reasons, none of which he cared to reveal on public television. "Let's just go with the original."

"This is super." Mang waved Gina closer. "Totally candid."

Jerry detested Mang's choice of words. Gina, and that thing inside of her, was as super and candid as a drive-by shooting.

"Stop!" he yelled.

Everyone ceased moving. The room paused for an explanation. The new and improved Jerry Nearing hunted for a quick answer—a single prescience of thought that made Gina disappear from sight and satisfy the crew. He dug his hands in his pockets and released a nervous laugh, which he quickly heard and ceased mid-yuk. Then he thought of a candid response of his own.

"Gotta go." Jerry exited the house and property, faster than it took Cortez to vanish into the trees.

His back pressed against the Porsche's form-fitting seat, as he raced out of the hills. He reached for his cell phone and dialed his lawyer, Ralph Tisch. He was the only man he knew who talked sense when he needed it.

CHAPTER 11

OPEN YOUR WALLET,
SHUT YOUR MOUTH

"This won't be as easy." Ralph Tisch sat with his feet on his desk. He'd just returned from St. Martin and sported the frankness and ease of a man disengaged from his everyday routine. "Not as easy as your divorce."

Jerry braced himself. Nothing felt harder than his divorce. He'd been talking with Gina for days and didn't like what he'd heard. "How do I know if Gina is carrying my child?"

"Could it be yours?"

"I only slept with her once."

"That's all it takes."

"I know."

"We can ask for ..."

Jerry's cell phone rang. He held up a finger to silence Tisch and brought the receiver to his ear. "Yes?"

"It's me, Chel."

"Chelsea." He'd been expecting her call.

"I received your invitation in the mail. So you want me to see that big project of yours."

He crossed his fingers, pulling his eyes away from the curious attorney. "It's nothing really, just the magic of television."

"I bet it's more than that. I'd like to see it."

"Good." He tried not to sound excited. The invitation was just for a visit. "Hey, how about I cook dinner? We can do it any day you'd like."

"You want to go to the trouble?"

"It's no problem."

"Are you sure?"

"How about Thursday, eight o'clock?" Jerry felt like a schoolboy, the one who held Chelsea's hand beside the creek in Chesterfield.

"I'll try my best."

He didn't like the word 'try.' Why couldn't she say yes or no? "We can do it another time."

"No, I want to come. I want to see the house."

"I'll whip up something easy."

"You don't have to."

"It's no trouble."

"Alright then, I'll see you at eight."

He listened to the line disconnect, fighting the urge to over-analyze the conversation. When did Chelsea become so complicated? She used to come right out with whatever she had on her mind. He needed to wrench her away from Cogdon.

When Jerry folded up the phone, Tisch was flipping through the financial page in the *Wall Street Journal*. "Are you ready now?"

"Sorry about that." Jerry stashed the phone in his blazer.

"There are choices, you know, paths to take."

Jerry'd forgotten where they were in the conversation. He buzzed in the afterglow of his chat with Chelsea. She had actually accepted his invitation to dinner. *Good deal. Double good deal.*

"A blood test can be deterministic," Tisch said.

"What kind of blood test?"

"On the baby." Tisch paused. "Gina Spagnoli's baby? The one that's supposed to be yours?"

"Oh, right." Jerry ripped himself from thoughts of his beloved Chelsea. "Will Gina do that?"

"Not without a subpoena."

"Let's do it."

"It will bring public attention. I guarantee that. I know her attorney."

"I don't want that." His thoughts returned to his dinner date with Chelsea. He hoped to build a chain of devotion that drew her back to his heart. "She can't find out about the baby."

"Who can't?"

"Anyone."

"You said *she*. Is there another woman involved?"

Jerry looked at Tisch as if he might read his mind. "No, I don't want anyone to find out. Do you hear me?"

"Okay?" Tisch sounded confused yet determined to execute his client's needs. It was all billable hours in the end. "I think I understand."

"No one can know about this."

"Then get ready to open your wallet."

CHAPTER 12

THE MISSING INGREDIENT

Late Thursday afternoon, the air felt warm for the small days of March. Jerry kept the kitchen windows ajar, as he rolled pasta dough upon the counter. The scents of Mascarpone and fresh cut parsley lent an alluring aroma to the kitchen. Cortez lapped water from a bowl in the expanded breakfast nook, and a woodpecker hammered the old pin oak beside the house.

Jerry stuffed fresh raviolis with cheese and spices and pinched the edges closed. He was building more than Chelsea's favorite meal. To create love from food, he required certain basic ingredients: Parmigiano, lemon, garlic, and olives. Breaded veal cutlets sat on paper towels near the burners, and spinach for the salad drained in a colander by the sink. His senses were more acute than ever. He imagined Chelsea across the table, taking his hand, undressing beside the dining room table. She liked to mix food with sex, complimenting his best work in the kitchen.

A puddle gathered on the ochre floor tiles near the cabinets, and as he carried the pasta to the refrigerator, his bare toes dipped into the water. He must have been careless and sloshed his glass. He bent down and mopped up the spill with a dishcloth.

He went to the sink and shook the spinach in the colander, but it wasn't dry enough. He returned to the island counter and spilled the walnuts on the cutting board. The thick nuts popped beneath his blade.

The puddle reappeared on the tiles. Jerry stared at it, thinking he'd discovered another spill, until he identified the source. The ceiling was leaking. A ring of water formed on the stucco ceiling, dripping down into the kitchen.

"No." He immediately thought of the old kitchen roof— the one Chelsea hounded him to fix—but this was new, and it hadn't rained for days. It must have been the pipes in the refinished master bath.

Jerry squeezed the phone in his fist. His current plumber was like any other that he hired. He was lucky to get the man on the line when he really needed help. "You've got to get over here."

"How bad is it?" The plumber sounded distracted, or was it disinterested?

"It couldn't be worse."

"Is it pouring out?"

"Any other part of the house could be leaking, and I wouldn't mind. Do you understand?"

"I'll try to get right on it."

"You must. I'll pay you anything."

Jerry heard the plumber hang up. He marched into the basement and meddled with the myriad of specially installed cutoff valves. It took him twenty minutes of running up and down the steps before locating the line for the master bedroom. He was behind schedule, and he still needed to buy wine.

He tacked a note for the plumber on the front door and aimed his Porsche toward Princeton. The car spun out on the driveway. *That leaky pipe better be history when I return.* He wanted no reminders of the past. He needed a spotless house and a stunning meal if he hoped to create magic.

The man at the wine shop counter wore a tunic top and a pair of bellbottom jeans. He sat on a stool and sipped latte, engrossed in a novel by Robert Gover. He bobbed his head, mumbling an occasional line from the book.

Jerry mulled through the dusty wine racks, listening to the man snort and laugh. He tried to grab the man's attention. "Where are the Italian reds?"

The man waved his hand without looking up. "Keep going."

"Where?"

"The middle front."

"Middle front?"

"Yes."

"Do you have Riserva Millennio?"

The man propped his glasses upon his head, annoyed by the interruption. One of his sandaled feet dropped to the floor. "What's that?"

"Riserva Millennio. It's a Chianti."

"Then it would be with the rest of the Italians."

"1985?"

"Sounds like a tasty year."

Jerry's cell phone began ringing, and he plucked it from his blazer. He noticed the counterman roll his eyes. "Hello."

"Jerry?" Chelsea's voice competed with a loud sucking sound in the background.

"Where are you?"

"Trenton Airport."

"Are you broken down?"

"No."

He recognized the gushing sound by Chelsea. It was the swirl of a jet engine turbine. "Are you picking someone up?"

"I hope this won't put you out."

"Are you going to be late?" *Good deal.* He'd get extra time to clean up the leak and prepare the vegetables.

"I'm going to have to cancel."

"Cancel?"

"I have special news. Haskell's proposed."

"Proposed what?"

"What do you think?"

It took a moment for the concept to hit home. It dropped down on him like one of those cartoon weights, the 500 pound iron block, the full out flattener. Now he heard a different gushing sound. It was the wind leaving his lungs.

"Jerry? Are you still there?"

"What did you tell him?"

"Yes."

His knees went weak. He propped himself against the doorframe of the wine shop. He'd been aced-out by that little creep again.

"I want your blessing." Chelsea sounded tentative.

My what?! "My blessing?"

"I want to be friends."

"Friends?"

"Jerry, you're repeating everything I'm saying."

"I am?"

"It's been more than a year since our divorce."

"Has it been that long?" He'd been counting too but for a different reason. He thought their time apart was too long. He gripped the doorframe, aware that the ground beneath him was shifting. "You're joking, right?"

"I'm boarding a plane for Mexico in a half hour. We'll be married at sunrise."

"Can you do that? Is that legal?"

"Haskell says that in Mexico you can get whatever you want, when you want it, fast."

"Are you going to live there?"

"I'm coming back. I'm sorry. I hope you didn't go to too much trouble for dinner."

"Well, I ... well, no."

"I knew you'd understand."

"Yes." That was him, always understanding. He wondered how he might be understanding and persuasive at the same time. It probably wasn't possible. That's how some men got everything. They took what they wanted. They weren't liked by others, but who cared?

"Can we reschedule when I get back?" she asked.

"Sure."

"Oh, and the house looks great. I watched every episode."

When she hung up, Jerry thought of the things he didn't say. He didn't bless her marriage, not to that moneygrubbing twerp. He didn't want her to go. He still loved her. *Don't do this!*

He saw his Porsche at the curb and hopped inside. He drove down Nassau Street, shifting up the gears. The engine growled. His tires crushed an empty soda can on the dividing line, spitting it out like a spent ammo cartridge. He ripped past the yield-to-pedestrian signs and thick white crosswalks, daring jaywalkers to cross his path. He gripped the gearshift and looked to the horizon, plotting a course for the airport.

As Jerry raced through the heart of town, people scattered to the sidewalks. A cyclist smashed into the bumper of a parked car and flipped. A lady with a baby stroller screamed at the top of her lungs. Jerry pushed down on the gas, pounding the horn, willing obstructions out of his path. A squad car jumped on his tail.

He swerved onto Mercer Street, running the traffic light. He nearly clipped the side of a mail truck. He was heading for the interstate highway, without really plotting a course. Red lights flashed in his rearview mirror. He'd smooth out his troubles at the airport. He needed to reach Chelsea before she lifted off the runway and out of his life forever. He'd pay any price to speak with her one last time.

Traffic slowed to a crawl. Jerry leaned on the horn, deciding to drive in the opposite lane. He weaved off the road to avoid oncoming cars. Dust flew up with bits of garbage in the shoulder. Car horns wailed, and brakes locked up. He smelled his clutch burning. He didn't care if the engine blew, as long as he reached the airport on time.

The police shouted through the PA system in their car. Jerry ignored their commands to pull over. He saw the open fields at Battlefield Park, as another squad car sped toward him in the shoulder. The chrome grille and fluttering lights bore down on his little sports car. For an instant, he imagined himself going head on and underneath the approaching car.

He cut the wheel and spun out on the lawn. Mud and hunks of sod sprayed his windows. He cut back several times to avoid people afoot. A man and dog leapt over a trashcan. One teenager paused before diving with her companions into the thorny bushes. Jerry lost control on the wet turf, stabbing at the floor for the brakes. His steering wheel felt loose in his palms; no traction at all. Trees and blue sky whirled past his eyes, but just as quickly, his tires took hold, and the Porsche jerked to a halt.

Two squad cars hemmed him in, front and back. Jerry hopped out and glanced over the Porsche's hood. By chance, he hadn't hit anyone or anything. Tire ruts extended from the road, a pair of serpentine trails leading back to the Porsche. A photographer stepped from a news van and snapped pictures.

The first policeman was a kid with his hair shaved like a boot camp marine. He started to yell without benefit of the PA. "What are you doing?"

Jerry stared at the crowd. He was dazed, catching his breath. His heart still pumped at full throttle, and he broke into a sweat. Something was wrong. There were too many people around for a weekday afternoon. How did they get here so fast?

"Alright, pal." the policeman yelled louder.

The second officer was older than Jerry. He had thick gray hair, like Haskell Cogdon. Jerry's problems blazed anew in his mind.

"Let him be," the senior officer said, noticing the bewildered look on Jerry's face. "He's not armed. He's not moving."

"Sir?" the senior officer asked. "Are you alright?"

Jerry saw the problem. The Mercer Oak was completely collapsed, split down the middle. Its colonial limbs sprawled across the lawn like a dead soldier. People carted away sections of bark and branches. A twisted limb poked from the back of a Subaru. Two kids dragged another branch. They'd been busy collecting souvenirs but stopped to watch Jerry.

The news photographer, on the scene to cover the fallen tree, had lucked into the moment. He snapped more pictures of Jerry beside his car. The flashbulb blinded Jerry, which was good because he no longer cared to see.

"What happened here?" Jerry asked.

The senior officer's gaze shuttled to the tree and back. "It's the oak."

"But what happened?"

"It fell last night. Didn't you hear about it?"

"Fell?"

"I suppose the windstorm took it down."

"They should've knocked it down years ago," the kid cop added. "What a waste of time it was saving this thing."

"It's gone?" Jerry just didn't grasp the facts.

He scanned the lawn as if he might find the tree somewhere else. Their tree—the spot where he and Chelsea shared countless picnics—was history, cut up and carted away for keepsakes. The sight mortified him, and his knees went weak again. He fell back against the hood of the Porsche.

"I can't believe it," he mumbled.

"It's just a tree." The senior officer approached Jerry, scanning the area around the car. He reached inside and nabbed Jerry's keys.

"It takes all kinds," the kid cop said.

The crowd chatted and laughed. Someone recognized the distraught millionaire as that guy from Home Makers, and the revelation spread quickly.

Jerry didn't care. He barely noticed the gawking and jeers. He put his face in his hands. Chelsea was gone, god-honest gone for good. He felt empty, hollowed out inside. He'd cry, but the tears were stuck. He'd become just like his father, incapable of expressing simple emotions, unable to recapture his heart.

"Sir?" The senior officer jangled a pair of handcuffs. "You should come with us."

Jerry dropped down further against his car, pressing his thumbs against his ears. In the back of his mind, he heard a terrible noise arching over the horizon. Jet engines roared overhead.

CHAPTER 13

THE WATCHTOWER

Tom and Dick gathered in dark trench coats on the cedar planks of Jerry's expanded front porch. A soft rain pattered the ground like crinkling cellophane. Jerry noticed Dick's leather briefcase. The men resembled Jehovah's Witnesses zoning in to ply their faith.

"We haven't seen you around lately." Dick met Jerry's eyes with sharp focus, as if calculating the exact placement before the door swung open.

Tom shuffled his shoes in a shallow puddle. He glanced up at the gray sky and blinked. His pock-marked face held the rain like tears. "What's going on, Jer?"

"Not much." Jerry was dressed in torn sweatpants and an old flannel shirt from his closet floor. He hadn't shaved in three days, and he'd just devoured a bland microwave hotdog. He lifted his shirtsleeve and wiped mustard from his mouth. In a pinch, the old flannel doubled as a napkin. "I didn't expect to see you guys up here."

"We were wondering what happened to you," Dick said.

"Nothing." *Absolutely nothing.* Jerry scratched his beard. The damp air felt strange against his skin. He hadn't been outdoors in days. He searched the horizon for Cortez. Where was that dog roaming in the rain?

"Can we come in?" Dick asked.

"I suppose."

The men stepped upon the antique rug in the foyer, pressing wet imprints in the gold and blue pineapple pattern. It was a rug that Chelsea had fallen in love with years ago in a Lambertville shop window, but she lacked the cash to bring it home. She spoke about it often, and Jerry was surprised when he found it still up for sale.

Tom hung his coat on a peg by the door. He raised his nose, like a plump gerbil testing the air. "What's that smell?"

"Dinner."

"Expecting company?"

"I just ate."

Tom scratched the roll of flab above his belt.

"Go check the kitchen," Jerry said. "There's leftover Chinese in the fridge and chips in the cabinet. Take whatever you find."

"Really?"

"Be my guest."

"Primo." Tom padded to the kitchen.

Jerry and Dick moved to the living room. Dick sat on a couch with flowered embroidery. The enormous piece of furniture had long sweeping arms and a scalloped back, yet beside the matching armchairs and the gaping hole of the stone fireplace, it wasn't as intrusive.

Dick was another issue. He offered sincerity, along with a healthy dose of inquisition. He often sported compassion that veiled enough pointed questions to run a Senate subcommittee hearing. "We're worried about you."

Jerry threw another log on the fire and sat down. "Who's worried?"

"The Winners Circle."

Jerry picked up the newspaper and spread it on the coffee table. Other unread papers piled on the dusty oak floor. Since Chelsea left for Mexico, he functioned outside the passage of time, shutout from the world. It didn't matter if the stock market, airplanes, or the house next door crashed to the ground. The oaks and maples budded in the valley. Jacob turned over the northern field for planting. The world spun in familiar cycles, yet without Jerry Nearing. He didn't even return Gina's phone calls about the baby. He just wrote checks to Tisch, telling him to 'handle it.'

"How's your son?"

Jerry caught Dick's stare and returned to the paper. "Oh, you heard about that."

"Tom told me. Have you seen him?"

"Gina sent a picture."

"Can I see?"

Jerry wasn't in the mood to sort through the stacks of mail on the kitchen counter. "It doesn't look like me."

"Babies don't look like anyone at first."

"This one doesn't look like me at all."

"What does the mother say?"

"We speak through attorneys."

"What does her lawyer say?"

"I'm financing Gina's condo in Princeton. She seems content with that."

"That's it? A condo?"

"What's your point?" Jerry turned the newspaper pages. He smelled the ink. It shaded his fingertips gray.

"Were you planning on coming back to us?"

"The Circle?"

"Yes."

He shrugged. "I don't know if it helps."

"Of course it helps." Dick opened his briefcase and thumbed through some paperwork.

Jerry wondered if Dick had prepared a speech. Even better, perhaps Dick was writing a book: *The Big Book of Dickisms, Meditations for the Financially Confused.* He could picture Dick selling CDs and videotapes—the whole vertical line of psycho-economic therapy—on late night cable TV.

"I have something to show you," Dick said.

Jerry continued to ignore Dick. Instead, he scanned the want ad section of the *Trentonian*. He didn't need anything. He was avoiding Dick's stare and hopefully the thrust of his argument.

Dull thuds emanated from the kitchen, like cartons hitting the tiles.

"Sorry," Tom said. "I'll put them back."

"Just leave them on the counter." Jerry perused the employment classifieds. It seemed like a lifetime ago when he culled this section for a nugget of hope.

"Hmm, Belgian chocolate," Tom mumbled. "Hey, Jerry? Can I have some of these?"

"Eat the whole box."

"Primo!"

Dick laid the paperwork on the coffee table. Colorful graphs and charts began crowding Jerry's newspaper. "I have it mapped out. You're caught in the denial phase."

"The denial phase?"

Dick landed a finger on a trough in the graph. There were crooked, intersecting lines, like those financial prospectuses that gave Jerry fits. "First you go through the crisis phase. That's when you win the money. There's euphoria, followed by the inevitable letdown. In the end, you realize everything's changed, but it may take a while."

"I know everything's changed, Dick."

"That's a great place to begin."

Jerry brushed aside the silly charts. "Chelsea used to do the same thing with our budget. The problem was we didn't have the cash flow to make it work."

"This isn't home economics. It's your life."

"Then why the charts?" He considered Chelsea's old projections for the future: a flush retirement fund, money for the kids' education, but income wasn't the issue anymore. He required a complete new set of goals.

"You need to rebuild your life."

No kidding. Jerry glanced around the living room in an attempt to deflect the obvious. "I've rebuilt my house."

"Seriously, you don't want to be like Tom before you figure things out."

"I'm not spending my money."

"You're not doing much of anything that I can see."

Jerry bit his lip. One more comment like that, and Dick was getting tossed out the door.

Dick retrieved the chart and slid his finger along the line. "Once you go through the acceptance phase, it's uphill."

Jerry stared at the pretty paper. Dick's plan sort of made sense, but Jerry needed to cut his last ties with Chelsea. That was the issue. He wondered if Dick brought a diagram for that. He didn't even want to admit those attachments still existed, yet if he salvaged a piece of his old life—a hobby, a talent, anything—it might fill the void. He considered Gina's baby boy. That didn't feel right either, and he didn't know why.

"I believe," Dick continued, "that regular appearances at the Winners Circle will help you heal."

"I figured you'd come to that."

"You must try."

"I'm not a millionaire."

"Oh, you're not?"

"Not like the others. I'm just a guy with money."

Dick laughed. "If I had a dollar for every time I heard that ..."

"It's true."

"If you're anything, you're a millionaire."

Jerry rubbed his temples. That's when he saw it staring him in the face, not one of Dick's pretty charts but a want ad in the newspaper. A company that he never heard of was starting up a parts manufacturing facility in the abandoned car plant. He seized the newspaper in both hands.

"What is it?" Dick leaned forward.

Jerry kept the paper close and read the small print. PTK Corp. needed men for the tool and dye line. His heart lifted. It was the right answer to a longstanding question. Who said a millionaire couldn't work? There'd be familiar faces along-side of him. He'd buy them lunch every day. He'd be a hero again.

"I've got it," he mumbled.

Dick craned his neck. "Got what?"

"My own solution." Jerry folded up the paper and tucked it in the drawer beneath the coffee table. He knew Dick was dying to see it, but he refused to let that happen.

"Have we met before?" Earl Breck studied Jerry's resume. He was the shop manager at PTK Corp., and he interviewed Jerry in a trailer beside the old car plant on Parkway Avenue.

A plane from the nearby Trenton Airport went overhead, rattling the flimsy aluminum walls. Jerry waited for the disruption to pass, staring through the plexiglass window at the hulking shell of the GM plant. The once proud building seemed a far cry from the plant that had manufactured fighter planes during WWII and rolled them down the streets toward the airport runway and cheering crowds.

"I don't think we've met." Jerry tugged at his starched collar. The suit and tie were too much. It made him appear desperate. Other applicants dressed in jeans and T-shirts—the stuff they'd be wearing to work.

"Your face looks familiar." Breck had a listing spine, as if he'd met up with more than his share of misfortunes on the manufacturing floor.

Jerry was certain he'd remember a man like that. "Did you work for GM?"

"No, PTK for twenty years, up in Somerville."

"I've never been to Somerville, I don't think."

"I know I know you. I'll get it."

"It's just a coincidence." Jerry squinted, hoping to make out the scribbles that Breck added to his resume. "So do I fit?"

"Your qualifications look right."

Good deal. "Then there's a slot for me?"

"Are you good on the fly? Sometimes these old machines breakdown."

"I used to tinker with them every week." Jerry straightened up, charged by the promise of steady work. On the line, his life made sense. The big machines shook the concrete floors. Hot grease and steam wafted through the air. He punched a card. He built things from raw materials. When it all came together, he was in a groove that lasted all day long.

"We'll be making parts for other machines." Breck looked up. He gave Jerry a double take and stabbed his pencil forward. "Breadbasket!"

"Excuse me?"

"Breadbasket, the homeless organization. You were at the annual auction."

Jerry recalled the event. It was a benefit for soup kitchens across New Jersey. Chelsea dragged him along, even though he loathed the buzz and glitz.

"You're that lottery man." Breck pushed aside the resume and sat back in his chair. "I was there. I volunteer for Breadbasket."

Jerry replayed the embarrassment in his head. He'd slapped a ten thousand dollar bid on a ceramic bust of Ronald Regan, hoping to satisfy Chelsea and create a quick exit, but the plan backfired, and the fledgling millionaire found himself in front of news photographers once again in gratitude for his generosity.

"What in the world are you doing here?" Breck asked.

"I want a job. I think I said that."

"Why?"

"Why not?"

Breck lowered his voice. "Did you blow the whole wad of cash?"

"No."

"Are you yanking me?"

"I'm serious."

"You're qualified, but ..." Breck motioned toward the waiting room, where men shuffled through stale copies of *Sports Illustrated* and *Time* magazine. "Can I explain it to them? There aren't enough jobs for everyone."

Jerry felt terrible. Breck was right. Jerry was being selfish. He wanted to slink from the office and retreat to the Hopewell hills. Forget about a job. What was he thinking?

"Since I have you here, Mr. Nearing." Breck's tone changed, no longer discerning the applicant before him. He got up and shut the door. "I have this idea."

"What is it?"

"Do you wear eyeglasses?"

"Not yet."

"Lucky son-of-a-bitch." Breck guffawed, his words meant as a compliment. "Don't get me wrong."

"I'm not getting you at all."

"Let me explain. What do you think of glasses without fingerprints?"

Jerry waited for the punch line. Was this a joke? Occasionally people became giddy around him, as if dollar bills might fly from his pocket if they made him laugh. For some unexplainable reason, he thought about reaching into his wallet and offering Breck a twenty for his trouble.

"That's right," Breck said, "smudge-free eyewear."

"I don't wear glasses."

"But lots of us do, and our lenses constantly have to be cleaned."

"I guess."

"Check these out." Breck pulled a pair of glasses from his pocket and plunked them in Jerry's hands. They were black frames, taped and glued in spots. The lenses appeared yellowed, like old dog's teeth.

Jerry turned them over, indulging the eager shop manager. He pictured himself in the parking lot, where his Porsche waited beside a collection of late model American vehicles and economy cars.

Breck leaned forward, blocking Jerry's exit from the chair. "You can get in on the ground floor. My buddy and me invented them. They're made of a special polymer. It resists the grease on a human hand."

"That's interesting."

"Great, huh?"

Jerry imagined his keys in the car's ignition. Breck repulsed him, especially the pushy attitude. Yes, coming here was definitely a bad idea.

"Try them," Breck said. "Press your fingers on 'em."

Jerry realized that he was mixing with the wrong people, and this bothered him, not that it was true but that he noticed it, sensed the difference. He was no longer one of those men in the waiting room. How many times had Dick tried to tell him?

"Go ahead," Breck pleaded. "Don't be shy."

Jerry pinched the lens between his finger and thumb. He held the glasses up to the light. He wasn't sure what he saw through the amber haze.

"Come on," Breck said. "Get your fingers all over them. You can't smudge 'em."

"Nope."

"What did I tell you? Un-smudge-able. Want in on the next great invention?"

"In?"

"My wife's developed a marketing plan. I think we can do the whole deal for under a million to start—plant, production, marketing, sales."

Jerry stood up and returned the glasses. "Let me think about it."

"Good. I have your number."

Jerry rushed through the trailer and pushed outside. Breck held onto the door, launching a final pitch for capital funds. Mercifully, a jet plane thundered overhead and deafened the rambling hole in Breck's face.

The Porsche waited beneath the sun like a big red bug with mag wheels. Jerry plodded forward. His steps were heavy. He felt more dejected than the day he received his pink slip.

He dropped into his car. Why didn't he see this coming? His perception was skewed. At the Winners Circle, people often blamed the lottery money for fostering a loss of reality. Money made you view the world as you wanted, not as it really was. Dick often reinforced this precept, but Jerry knew the true reason behind his own lack of clarity. A rattlesnake had altered his brain cells, and a slick of venom still pulsed through his veins, tainting every thought he conceived.

CHAPTER 14

THE WINNERS ALLIANCE

"Who wants to comment on that?" Dick commanded room 201B at the Trenton JCC. He scanned the faces in the circle of plastic chairs, slapping his pen in his palm. He resembled a well-dressed prison guard pressing for answers. "Tom thinks he's better off without the money."

"I don't think being broke is the answer." Jerry fanned away Arlene's cigarette smoke. It burned his eyes.

"I'll second that." Arlene puffed again. A thin tube of ash bent from the tip of her cigarette, like a charred tree limb. She was spending a little too much time at the tanning salon, and her skin glowed with a queer orange hue.

"Don't get me wrong. I still believe in money." Tom sat by the window, noshing on a chocolate éclair. Since the loan to repurchase his father's bakery fell through, he adopted a cavalier attitude about wealth.

"What is it that you believe?" Dick flipped through his notebook.

"I still believe it can make good."

"That's great. You must keep the faith."

"I want more money. I hope to have it one day."

"And you will. Be positive."

"But I don't know if I need millions. I've done that."

Jerry considered the lottery tickets in his wallet. He still purchased them, just like the old days. He bought a strip of five from Mojique at the Seven-Eleven, plus an extra large cup of black coffee. The ritual made him feel like a regular guy, but he'd never confess it to this crowd.

Tom swallowed a huge mouthful of pastry. You almost saw it slide down his gullet. "I tried to guess where I went wrong, so I traced things backwards."

"Excellent," Dick said. "Go with that thought."

"I was happy before I won the money, but if I had the choice again, would I give it away from the start?"

Jerry chewed on that question. He'd given half of everything to Mel Cogdon. Unfortunately, it was the half that he wanted to keep. Chelsea never phoned. She never sent e-mail. It'd been a month, and not even a postcard from Mexico dropped out of his mailbox. He anticipated one of those tacky honeymoon pictures with her and Mel donning oversized sombreros—the lovebirds in goofy bliss. He'd prepared himself not to react, but he never thought that no contact might bother him more.

Arlene tapped her ash into a plastic cup. "You should make a checklist: good points on the right, bad points on the left. See how it adds up."

Tom wiped his mouth with a napkin. "On one hand, I liked being able to have choices, but on the other, there's that constant worry about what to do."

"Correct," Dick said. "Freedom has its price."

"I've decided that I would give the money away, donate it to charity."

"Stop it!" Jerry thumped his heel on the linoleum floor.

The room turned abruptly toward Jerry.

"That's ridiculous," he said. "You wouldn't give the money away."

Tom looked hurt. This happened once per session, but usually Dick told him off. "Yes. I, I ..."

"You're broke because nobody stopped you from making bad choices." Jerry had had enough of this. He suddenly understood the term 'oral masturbation.' If Tom wanted to dream aloud, he should take up a writing career.

"But ..."

"But nothing. You got rich, then spent it all. It's that simple."

"I guess I invested cash in the wrong areas."

"You thought the money was the answer to your problems. You thought you could buy the answers."

"I didn't know what I was doing."

"That's my point. No one told us what to do. No one warned us what might happen."

The room fell silent. Every man and woman in the circle acknowledged Jerry's words with a long glance or a nod of the head. He felt like a teacher who just scolded the class. It was a red-hot poker of truth in the eye, the poignancy searing, concrete enough to touch, and who'd dare refute it. Everyone already knew the truth. In fact, they lived it. They came to the Winners Circle for affirmation of the facts.

Jerry noticed Dick squinting in his direction. Jerry recognized that look too. Dick's big brain was turning. Dick had a new idea.

A week later, Dick planted himself in the middle of Jerry's Victorian couch. He and Tom were making a habit of showing up unannounced at the farmhouse, but this time, Dick was on an urgent mission. He bent Jerry's ear for twenty minutes. He plotted to save the world, at least their part of it. He was going to shield the big dollar lottery winners from harm and especially themselves.

"Something tells me you have a name for this plan," Jerry said.

"It's called the Winners Alliance." Dick donned a content expression, as if he'd just laid out the inner workings of the first atomic bomb and given it a name. "I took the idea from you. We're going to warn them. We're going to warn them all."

"We can't warn them."

"We can, and we will."

Jerry was speechless. It was impossible to warn anyone about the future, much less predict its color and shape in advance. He'd tried it once and ended up with something that resembled nothing he'd imagined. "What about the Winners Circle?"

"The Circle's still going on. We'll always need that to mop up broken lives. This is a splinter group to counteract problems before they start."

"Who's in it?"

"Just us—you, I, and Tom. Tucker will perform the undercover work." Dick leaned closer, as if someone bugged their conversation from outside the room. "I want no one else to know. It's a secret alliance, a sub-entity within the Winners Circle."

"This all seems a little too covert for me. Explain it again."

"We monitor millionaires for signs of personal and financial destruction, then intervene at the right moment."

Jerry worried whenever Dick got to thinking like this: the plans, the secrets. "How will you know when the right moment arrives?"

"Tucker's putting a file together on everyone."

"Everyone?" Jerry scanned Dick's dark priest-like getup. Dick was a zealot for sure, noble but naïve, not to mention a little scary, the essence of a true missionary. One hundred years earlier, he'd be roaming the jungles, converting natives to Christians, and as always with a zealot, it was mostly about the converter as opposed to the converts.

"Everyone in the last ten years will have a file," Dick said. "We'll review them regularly for changes. They'll be a file on each of us as well. It's the only fair way."

"I suppose." Jerry heard Tom rummaging in the kitchen. The teakettle boiled and a package of potato chips or pretzels ripped open. "What does Tom think?"

"He's in."

"Just like that?"

"Yes."

"He's not nervous?" Jerry knew what a worrywart Tom was.

"The Alliance will pay him a stipend for odd jobs and driving."

"Oh, that's why he's in."

Dick ignored the remark. "What do you say? Are you joining us?"

"You really need me for this?"

"There's a presence about you."

"I'm not roughing anyone up."

"You're solid, Jerry." Dick slapped him in the arm, as if the threesome were embarking on a rugby scrum instead of something weird and outrageous.

"No funny stuff?"

"Nothing unnecessary."

Jerry looked at Dick's outstretched hand. He was bored silly, rattling around the farm from sunup to sunset. What was the harm? A phone call here; a letter there. Besides, he needed the companionship. "Alright, I'll see how it goes."

"Great." Dick pulled a file from his loaded briefcase and dropped it on the coffee table. "You're our first case."

"You're joking."

"Do I joke?"

Jerry just stared. *No, you have no sense of humor whatsoever.*

"Gina Spagnoli," Dick said. "How much money have you spent on her?"

"I don't know. Twenty, thirty grand. I have to check with Tisch."

"Do you even know if it's your child yet?"

"No, not yet. I mean, I assume it is."

"You assume?"

"Yes." He noticed how weak that sounded. So much for having the 'presence' that Dick had metioned.

Dick conjured that hit man look in his eye. A fresh idea was forming. "I think it's time we found out for a fact or not if that baby is yours."

CHAPTER 15

INCIDENTAL BABY

"Is this the best way?" Jerry sat in the back seat of Dick's navy blue Lincoln Navigator. Tom drove, and Tucker rode shotgun. Jerry nudged Dick in the elbow. "Are you sure we can't speak to Gina first?"

"She'll never agree to it." Dick was dressed in his black uniform—turtleneck, linen slacks, Milanese loafers. He had the Winners Alliance files spread on his lap, studying a floor plan of Gina's new condo in the Princeton borough. "We need results, not to mention discretion. And the Spagnoli woman is incapable of both."

"I don't know how discrete this will be."

"More discrete than a public court battle, and you don't want that. Millionaires lose in the public eye. Spagnoli understands that and is using it against you. The press will turn you into Leona Helmsley and dig you a grave."

"It won't go that far."

"I'm telling you, get the blood specimen from the child. A gene test will eliminate you as the father with 99.9 percent accuracy."

"What if I just sit down with her and ask for a sample?"

"I expect a suggestion like that coming from Tom."

Tom rolled his eyes in the rearview mirror. Tucker snickered.

"There has to be another way," Jerry said.

"We've been over this. We can't uncover the child's medical records, not even the pediatrician's name. The Spagnoli woman has got the child's information clamped down like Fort Knox gold."

"That's for sure."

"She must be under guidance. My guess is her lawyer is excellent."

"That's what my attorney said."

"Don't doubt it. Tucker tried bribing the records office in town. It was like the child didn't exist."

"I saw Gina. She was as plump as a Thanksgiving turkey." Jerry glanced at the color blowup of the baby—bruised and abused from delivery. A swirl of black hair covered his head, much like his own at birth. He sighed. This was his relation-ship with his son: paychecks out, pictures back in the mail. The level of communication wasn't much better than with his old man. "Damn."

"Take it easy," Dick said. "Just follow the plan, and we'll straighten out this mess."

"What if it really is my child?"

"I've got a plan for that too."

Jerry hesitated to hear it but knew he would anyway. Dick loved the sound of his own voice, especially when he had an idea, which he always did.

"The Alliance will take care of everything," Dick said. "This is only phase one. Phase two, if necessary, will be to get your son away from the Spagnoli woman."

"Let's stick to phase one for tonight, if you don't mind."

"I'll review, so there's no confusion. When Tom and Tucker create the diversion, go in the opposite direction with the child. Create time and space between you and Spagnoli."

"This better work."

"We've got sirens, bomb explosions, the works." Dick glanced at the huge speakers in the payload compartment. They looked like walnut veneer replicas of the Washington Monument. They were unable to stand up straight in the truck. "We bought Tucker a new stereo."

"One thousand watts, mate." Tucker grinned, his big ears fanning from his head like open sails. "Can't wait to plug her in at home."

"At a minimum, Spagnoli will run to the window to check it out," Dick said. "That'll give you time to duck out the rear. Later on, tell her you retreated to protect your son. Who would blame you?"

"Okay." Jerry pulled the blood stick from his pocket.

"Stick the kid and tuck it away," Dick said. "We don't need a lot."

"That's the part I hate."

"It's simple. You practiced a dozen times on Tom last night."

Tom waved his hand above the steering wheel. The band-aids on his fingertips flashed beneath a passing streetlight.

"Alright. I can do this."

"That's the spirit." Dick slapped Jerry's shoulder and turned toward the front seat. "Men, pull over at the next corner."

Gina came to the door in a pink negligee with a satin shawl. Jerry's eyes fell to the aureole of her left breast peeking from the lacy material. She appeared trim and energetic, yet she'd given birth only a few months earlier.

"Hello, Gina," Jerry said.

She allowed him a moment to stare, before whipping the shawl over her chest. "Excuse me. I was just feeding your son."

"How's little Jerry doing?"

"You can see for yourself." She tugged down on the lapels of his jacket, forcing him to bend. She rose to the tips of her bare toes and kissed him on the cheek. "I'm glad you came."

"I phoned you on short notice. I hope it's not too late."

She sparkled. "We've been waiting up for you."

Gina led him down the hall to the room beside the master bedroom. Jerry reviewed the floor plan in his head. Gina occupied the first floor. When the diversion struck, he was to exit near the patio. It was a warm spring night. She might not hear the baby cry or even notice him missing.

The nursery was azure blue with puffy clouds sponged on the upper walls and ceiling, which pleased Jerry in a way he couldn't name. Gina dipped her arms into the crib and removed the swaddled child.

Jerry held his breath. The infant's dark hair was gone, replaced by a smooth scalp with scant flecks of dried skin. A little hand with tiny fingernails poked from the powder blue blanket and pawed Gina's chest. Jerry had handled the same breast on a couple of occasions. How strange was life?

"Here's your boy." Gina set the baby in Jerry's arms.

His shoulders drew tight, and his arms went stiff. He feared he might drop the child, but the soft bundle weighed nothing at all.

He tugged the blanket from the baby's chin and stared at the little nose, eyes, and mouth. The baby latched onto Jerry's finger. It felt warm and firm. He caught an unusual sweet scent, as his own emotions beset him. He thought his eyes might tear but resisted the feeling.

"What do you think?" Gina asked, beaming as if she'd produced the little masterpiece all by herself.

"He's so small."

"He's already put on three pounds."

"Three?"

"He'll gain a lot more with your genes."

"I hope you can forgive me. I never meant for this to happen."

"I know you. You're a decent man. You'll do the right thing."

Jerry found her face. Paying money wasn't a lot to ask. He had millions, most of which remained untouched by his Spartan ambitions. "I'll do everything I can."

A sharp explosion echoed in the street. At first, he forgot about the diversion. He clutched the baby harder, noticing the panicked look on Gina's face.

"Oh my God." Gina bolted from the room.

Jerry watched her disappear down the hall. He stood, dumbfounded by the excellence of Dick's plan.

The baby's eyes were wide-open, staring back at the big man above. The child's eyes seemed to be saying: *It worked! You're crazy friends pulled it off. It actually worked.*

Little Jerry kept staring. *You're supposed to run now, silly.*

Jerry rushed for the exit, with the baby tucked in one arm like a football. He zigzagged through the halls, dodged a standing lamp near the corner, and located the den at the back of the condo. He slipped through the back door and onto the patio in the dark, thrilled to hit his destination on target.

Little Jerry didn't seem to mind. He enjoyed the motion, cooing at daddy.

Jerry shut the door and whipped out the blood stick. He heard Dick's words, 'Stick the child and forget it. It's done a million times a day, in thousands of hospitals.' He hoped it didn't hurt the little guy.

The sound of explosions reverberated from the front. Little Jerry blew bubbles. Jerry opened the sterile package and jabbed the stick into the baby's palm.

The child began wailing in accordance with the bombs.

Jerry grabbed the doorknob, but it didn't turn. "Not one of those."

He glanced the length of the building. The condos spread out like a prison wall, redundant and unscalable yet adorned with a variety of patio furniture, barbecue grills, and the odd bicycle. He slid the blood sample into the plastic sleeve and ran for the front.

Bombs continued to burst, echoing throughout the complex. As he rounded the building, he nearly tripped over a stray garden hose and counted his blessings. He reached the front lawn, holding the child close, protecting him against the noise, but the explosions suddenly ceased.

He stopped and rocked little Jerry. The baby wailed like a bad dream.

"It's okay." He rocked softer and then faster. He was as suited to this business as being a millionaire. "Please, it's okay. It's okay."

The noise of car wrecks supplanted the suburban warfare. From Tucker's new monster stereo, the peaceful neighborhood was treated to a concert of screeching tires, crashing metal, and shattering windshields. The baby achieved a crescendo of cries between gasps for air.

Amid the worst of it, Jerry heard Tucker and Tom arguing. This particular change of diversionary tactic wasn't in their plans.

Jerry headed toward the Navigator. The men shoved each other by the open trunk. Dick was mediating, while pressing buttons on the stereo's main console. The cassette tape flipped over, and the sound of barking dogs punched through the huge speakers.

"Hey!" Jerry yelled, rocking the baby. "Cut the noise already!"

He stood in the middle of the street, screaming at his partners. He was afraid to approach Tucker's watt-guzzling stereo system with the baby. He cupped one hand over the baby's ears, waving the other to seize their attention. "I've got it already."

Heads poked from windows in the shell-shocked complex. Two men wandered onto their lawns. Dogs barked and howled. Jerry considered retreating into Gina's condo, leaving the fearless trio to whatever end befell them.

Then he saw the dogs.

A rottweiler, with massive haunches and a head like the working end of a front-end loader, tore down the pavement. It appeared disturbed by the noise, bearing down on the tall screaming man who flapped his arm in the street like an out of control water pump. Two dachshunds followed the bigger dog, their long bodies waggling like balloon animals with feet.

Jerry stopped yelling and lowered his arm, but it appeared too late to slow the dogs. He watched the charging animals, shuffling through his options like a bad hand at a poker game. He decided to fold, running in the opposite direction. He'd handle any dog alone. Cortez was big, and Jerry could wrestle that animal down, but not with the baby, not with little Jerry.

The German dogs kept pace behind him. The rottweiler ran well out in front. The dachshunds were one thing. He'd stamp them out with his shoes if needed, kick them clear across the road, but the rottweiler formed another problem, and Jerry had only one free arm.

He leapt over the hedges and flowerbeds. The German breeds followed. The rottweiler hurdled the gardens, while the dachshunds trod through the greenery and mashed the pansies without much pizzazz.

Condo Block C lay several yards ahead. Jerry searched for a safe spot—a place with elevation. Forget the stairs. That big dog might corner him there.

The Germans closed the gap, as the bomb bursts returned. Jerry spilled over a chainlink fence, careful to keep little Jerry unharmed. His shoulder slammed the cement surface, and he braced his legs against a steel patio table to stop rolling. He saw the aqua blue ripples of a swimming pool lit up at night.

Jerry stood up. The Germans penetrated the pool yard. The rottweiler cleared the fence, tumbling to a halt, while the dachshunds squeezed through the gate like rats. He jumped onto the patio table and hoped for the best.

The rottweiler galloped to the table, scraping its paws upon the cement. Jerry waited for the powerful dog to spring off its paws. He crouched, preparing to dart in any direction, but the dog stopped short, releasing a growl that rivaled Tucker's stereo.

The dachshunds mounted the chairs and hopped upon the tabletop. Jerry shifted his weight, sensing his precarious stance. The table teetered and moaned. It wouldn't be long before the whole thing toppled and he was into the shallow end of the pool, holding poor little Jerry above the water.

Not surprising, the smaller dachshund was the most aggressive. It latched onto the cuff of Jerry's chinos and tugged, snarling like a big house cat.

Jerry stood on one foot, shaking his leg. The table wobbled. The baby wailed. The rottweiler growled like a diesel engine. Jerry shook his leg in a crazy dance, but the dachshund hung on.

He whipped the blood stick from his blazer and stabbed the little animal in the rump, drawing another sample into the mix. The dachshund yelped and hopped backward. He stuck the other dachshund head on, lancing it in the front quarter like a bull in an arena.

The pesky duo leapt off the table, retreating for the gate. He watched them fighting to squeeze through first.

But the rottweiler stayed on, drooling at the foot of the table. It clawed the cement, jerking its head with each mighty bark, spraying saliva upon the metal chairs and corrugated cement.

Jerry gently placed the infant on the center of the table. He noticed the baby wriggle on the cool metal. "I'll protect you."

He stepped down. With both hands free, he was a different piece of meat to master.

The rottweiler leveled a nasty look on Jerry. Nothing much in its dark inset eyes resembled sanity. Sometimes a normal dog got worked into a frenzy and past the point of reason, yet a rottweiler was no normal dog. It weighed one hundred pounds, capable of bringing most men to the ground. And that was no place to be with a dog like this.

They circled each other beside the pool. Reflections from the water rippled across the dog's blue-black fur and its lumpy head. Jerry heard the baby crying and discovered his own rage.

He picked up a chair and smacked the dog's side. It lunged for the fat part of his calf, and he kicked the big animal with the toe of his pointed wingtips, separating a chunk of flesh above its eye. *These shoes are good for something.*

The rottweiler looked angrier, if that was possible, slobbering sticky strings of saliva upon anything close by. It growled a base tone, hunching down, but after a few more cracks of the chair and stabs of Jerry's pointy shoe, the big man backed the dog near the white coping of the pool.

He knew one thing about this sort of fight: no mercy. He rammed the chair into the dumb animal with all of his strength and shoveled it into the drink.

A splash of water rose and fell. The rottweiler surfaced and paddled in the water, fighting to pull itself over the coping.

Jerry smacked his heel across its snout, dunking it back under the water. He watched the rottweiler's fat head get wet, and he repeated this until the dog's spirit appeared broken. He enjoyed it more than he thought. He even felt like smacking the dog's owner a couple of times too.

A set of recessed steps lay at the shallow end of the pool. Jerry stood over the defeated animal churning in the water. "Figure it out for yourself."

He retrieved the child from the table. The dog thrashed in the background.

The dachshunds lingered beyond the gate, but as soon as they spotted Jerry, they vanished through the hedges, yelping into the night. He thought he saw the blood stick still poking from one of the dogs.

He found the street and regained his breath. He was scuffed up and dirty. He bled from a scrape in his palm and where his pants tore through at the knee. Little Jerry cried and gasped. Thank God, the sound effects had ceased. Jerry cradled the unharmed child, setting his sights on the parking lights of Dick's Navigator.

The police were interrogating the members of the newly formed Winners Alliance. The cops blocked the street, listening to Dick's fast-talk about the stereo. Jerry heard Dick turning the questions back on the cops, like only Dick knew how. Tucker and Tom hung nearby, idling like coats on a rack. But after everything that had just happened, Jerry only chuckled at the sight.

The police appeared more befuddled than disturbed. Jerry understood their confusion. Here were three normal-looking men in a quiet upscale neighborhood, blasting doom from a huge stereo like a posse of rap gangstas on holiday.

"My baby!" A woman in jeans and a Mickey Mouse sweatshirt sped toward Jerry. Her arms were outstretched, and her long brown hair waved behind her.

Jerry held the boy tight. *Now what?*

"Hold up!" Gina tried to intercept the stranger. She approached in her shawl and negligee, shuffling her pink slippers with as much grace and speed as she could muster. She slunk across the pavement, like a fashion model trying not to sprint down the runway while making good time.

"Oh God, my baby!" The woman cried.

Jerry realized the woman was headed straight for him. He stopped walking. The child whined and wriggled in his arms. "Your baby?"

The strange woman's eyes were a bit too close together, kind of like Gina's. She pawed at the baby. "You found him."

"He wasn't lost." Jerry stepped back. "I had him the whole time."

Gina wedged in between, palming the woman further back. "Calm down."

"Give me Anthony," the woman pleaded.

"Anthony?" Jerry twisted away, as the woman reached again. "His name is Jerry. Who are you?"

Dick's ears perked up. He pulled away from the cops. "I knew it!"

Jerry peered down on Gina. "Who is this lady?"

"My cousin." Gina threw her foot, smacking the other woman in the ankle. "She's very attached to the child."

Gina's cousin ceased talking. She formed a crooked smile. Red blotches covered her neck and one cheek.

"She said this is her baby." Jerry was indignant.

"Oh, did she?" Gina's hard fought composure eroded. "Whatever. Give me little Jerry."

"She called him Anthony. Why would she say that?"

"Don't you get what's going on here?" Dick got in Gina's face. "You're a despicable woman. You don't have a child, do you?"

Gina looked a little green, a bad contrast against all that pink lingerie. "Who the heck are you?"

"I'm your worst nightmare." Dick lived for these moments. He eyed Gina like a thief cornered with the good silver. He planted his feet on the blacktop and folded his arms across his chest. He seemed ready to sick Tucker on her.

She released a little laugh, testing the crowd to see who followed, and when Jerry kept staring, she tugged her shawl tight to her chest and launched into recovery mode. "It's not as bad as it looks."

Gina's cousin swallowed her stupid expression and yanked the baby from Jerry's grip. She held the infant to her chest, and he quieted and shut his eyes.

"An old fashioned con," Dick announced, as if anyone needed a summary. "Well, you're blown out of the water, sister, completely exposed."

Jerry turned away, disgusted. A minute earlier, he was rescuing his son, but as usual, it was for nothing. He had no son, no legacy to guide toward a better future. It was another disappointment. Another loss. Another bit of fake to fill up his soul. When there seemed to be no more pieces left of his heart to rip out, Gina had found another, fished it out and served it up to him. He was nauseated by the idea of having to swallow this too.

"Okay," Gina said. "So you don't want a child. I read you all wrong."

Jerry clenched his jaw. He started walking with no specific direction in mind. If there was an arrow in the sky pointing 'somewhere else,' Jerry might follow it.

"I was only giving you what you wanted," she continued.

"Spagnoli," Dick said, "you're lucky if he doesn't press charges."

If the cops weren't confused before, their brains twisted into knots now. They clearly regretted answering this call. They edged toward their squad car, hoping for another emergency to blare over the dispatch—a burning building, a bloody car wreck, anything to escape the loony tunes at the Princeton condos.

Gina followed Jerry for a few paces. "Jerry, please."

Jerry kept moving.

"You just can't sleep with a woman and abandon her."

Jerry didn't even glance back. *Shut up. You got paid like everyone else.*

Twenty minutes later, Dick's Navigator pulled beside Jerry as he meandered down the highway. The custom tires ground the dirt and glass in the roadside.

"Hello," Dick called from an open window. His blithe tone signaled victory. The others were laughing. Tucker sipped a large can of beer, probably a Foster's Lager.

Jerry didn't have the stomach for celebration. He assumed that they'd cleared up their trouble with the cops, but he still felt as snake-bit as ever. He was a man with so-called options, but the world shut its doors as fast as he reached for them. "What do you want?"

"Well," Dick said, "I'd call that a success."

"Excuse me."

"Chalk up one for the Alliance."

CHAPTER 16

HORSE'S NECK

For days, Jerry kept to himself. He drove along the peaks and valleys of the Sourland Mountains, tight in the cocoon of his highly tuned imported racing machine. The hardwood forests whipped past his windows. The spawning foliage blurred his sightlines and tented his thoughts.

He slowed his car outside Taddler's Horse Center. Purple and white violets peppered the sprawling lawns. He retracted the car roof and studied the corrals and barns from a distance. He'd stopped three times that week, but today, a gentle breeze pushed the scent of horses, trodden earth, and straw-covered manure to the roadside. He decided to pull up the driveway.

A dozen horses strolled the western paddock. Jerry counted the trailers lined up for the weekend horse show. Wasn't this the life he wanted? Hadn't he dreamt of this before striking it rich? A barrier existed between his poverty and wealth, between his past and present. It created a myth of his past, which was now as fleeting and hard to prove as a lie. He tried to trace his fantasies to the other side, but they were impossible to imagine when they became reality with the mere tearing out of a bank check.

The Porsche mounted the crest of the hill in second gear. In the old days, his rickety Ford barely reached the top. He gazed down on the main barn. He planned to speak with the owner. He wanted to be a horse trainer. He was going to learn how.

A taupe mare strolled beside the fence. Its light eyes focused on Jerry, before it galloped into the pasture. Jerry thought of Chelsea. She possessed the body of a horse: slender neck, strong legs, fluid strides. She had a runner's form, full of grace when she believed no one was watching. She'd have taken naturally to a horse. Now he remembered the dream. He was going to teach her how to ride. They'd grow old watching their children on horseback. That was it.

The Porsche rolled downhill. He coasted in, sneaking up on the activity. The huge barn doors were drawn aside, as the handlers groomed the big animals. He knew nothing of this work, and his resume spoke of even less experience. Already he heard their questions. Who are you? Why do you want to do this?

He stopped not far from the spot where the rattlesnake first pierced his veins. A tremor of excitement charged his spine. He neared the center of his universe—a place of dreams and nightmares, the vortex of change.

A few handlers glanced, as he rose from the car. Did they remember? Some probably did.

"Morning," he called. He waited, but no one answered.

Dozens of people roamed the barn. The horse show began in three hours, and the breezeway teemed with professionals and avid fans of the breed. Two men inquired about registration and schedules. A lame colt waited for assistance.

"Sir?" A young woman from the barn clutched a bridle in one hand. The buckles jangled on the straps.

"Hello," Jerry said.

"You can't park here."

"I'll bring it up to the house. Is Sam Taddler around?"

"He's very busy."

Jerry realized it was the same woman who'd phoned the ambulance on the day he was bitten by the snake. She didn't recognize him in designer clothes and a perfect haircut. His hands were clean, and his glimmering car looked as if it were bathed more often than an infant.

"Hey," Jerry said in an odd way, trying to jog her memory.

"Are you showing today?" She looked past him for a truck and trailer, anything to indicate that he belonged.

"No, not today."

"Well maybe you should try back during the week."

Jerry stood by the open door of his car. Perhaps his former life wasn't real. He scanned the pasture for a memory of his own, only spotting the taupe mare. She grazed in the heather grass, flagging her tail.

"Sir?"

He saw men and women walking about the fields. They moved with purpose, watering horses, assembling the color-coded steeples for the competition. He understood their motivation, because he'd once wielded that kind of confidence and determination. He used to rise in the morning and knew what needed to be done. He'd felt every task calling him, even the menial tasks that supported the others, and it never fazed him or pressured him into mistakes. But today, he'd pulled into the horse center on nothing more than a whim. He'd become one of those millionaires that he used to mock, a man who thought he could walk among the working stiffs and cause them to stand at attention, even care about his concerns. His transformation was complete.

"You'll have to move your car," the woman said.

He didn't answer, and although his feet hadn't budged, he was already backing up. *No, you can't let a manure shoveler train horses, even a filthy rich manure shoveler.*

"Your car, sir?"

Jerry ducked inside his overpriced indulgence for transportation. He saw the mare in the distance. It seemed like a far off point on the horizon, beautiful, intangible. "I was just leaving."

CHAPTER 17

THE WEALTHY
WILLIE NELSON

A damp wind whistled through a crack in the window, as the Winners Alliance sped toward Cape May—the bottom tip of New Jersey. After the debacle at Gina's, Jerry swore he'd never rejoin the Alliance, but three weeks later, he was buckled into Dick's Navigator for another mission. Everyone understood why. It'd been two years since Jerry struck it rich, and his life was emptied out like a used box of cereal. He needed an excuse to lower his feet out of bed in the morning.

"It's an intervention," Dick said in his Gordon Liddy kind of way.

"I guessed as much." Jerry kept tabs on each winner in the files. He'd begun reluctantly but became fascinated with the twists and turns of the other millionaires' lives. He knew about the woman in Bridgewater who was obsessed with handbags and Latin lovers. A young couple who lived on a ranch at the Water Gap were forming their own religion, and of course, there was Chelsea and Haskell Cogdon. "Which case is it?"

"It's Willie Nelson."

"I thought so," Jerry replied. He and Dick formed the brains of the Alliance. Dick conjured the grand schemes, and Jerry added the commonsense, he hoped.

"He's stockpiling guns."

"I'm not surprised." Jerry sorted through Tucker's recon photos. Willie Nelson wasn't the famous singer, just some guy with nutty parents who named their kid after a country music star. Seven months ago, Super Pick Millions remade Willie into a rich and bitter winner. One photo showed him emerging from an army-navy store in Voorhees with three rifles.

Jerry called to the front. "What's that I smell?"

"Linzer Tart." Tom sampled desserts from an Atlantic City bakery. He planned on returning to the business as soon as he gathered the capital.

"Any good?" Jerry encouraged Tom's plans. He'd lend Tom the money, if he didn't think the hapless dreamer would turn it into a bagels-by-airmail franchise and lose every dime. Hell, he might lend him the cash anyway.

"I've had better pastries," Tom said.

"Pass me something."

Tom held the white box above the seat. He turned his chunky nose from the wheel and shot a sarcastic glance at their leader. "Try the Napoleon, Dick."

Dick ignored him.

Jerry reached for a clamshell pastry and bit into the flaky dough. The rich lemon custard evoked old memories. Chelsea and he occasionally splurged on fancy desserts or part of a gourmet meal. They'd spread the good china on the living room floor and light candles. Now that he had the means to eat with style, he ate quickly, standing in front of the TV. Last night, he gulped down a frozen microwave dinner: Cajun Shrimp with Savory Potatoes. It tasted like the cardboard and plastic in which it was packed.

Dick stroked his chin. He loved to add mystique to an already sketchy situation. "Our source tells us that Willie Nelson is about to hit a sour note."

"Great," Jerry said, devoid of emotion.

"He's planning to send anyone who ever crossed him On The Road Again, if you catch my drift."

"Yeah," Tom said, "but with a one-way Ticket to Ride."

"That's the Beatles," Jerry said.

"What?" Tom glanced into the rearview mirror.

"'Ticket to Ride.'"

"What are you talking about?"

"Forget it," Dick said. "Stay on the subject."

Tucker snickered and scooped a handful of cookies from the box.

Jerry pulled Chelsea's file from the briefcase and flipped through the pages. Haskell Cogdon was in trouble with the IRS and a few state agencies. The whole mess centered on a bad real estate deal in the Pine Barrens, but Jerry didn't need the Alliance for that information. The newspapers ran a story almost every day.

Dick held a furtive look in his eye. "Still keeping up with Joneses?"

Jerry closed Chelsea's file. "I can't help myself."

"Did you catch his real name?"

"Melvin?"

"Melvin Cogdon. Not as aristocratic as Haskell Cogdon. No wonder he changed it."

"No wonder." Jerry felt sorry for Chelsea. She still had no children, and her life was more imperfect than ever. Neither one of them got exactly what they bargained for.

Dick waved Willie Nelson's file in the air. "Can we stick to business?"

"Sure."

"I think we can make headway here."

"What are we going to do?" Jerry waited for him to suggest a phone call, but they'd traveled too far down the Garden State Parkway for that. A sign for Cape May raced past the window: 15 miles. They were heading toward something big—Dick's most ambitious plan to date. Since the moment the Alliance formed, Jerry felt this day coming. Dick needed to get it out of his system.

"We're doing what we set out to do." Dick brushed back his coat jacket, revealing a handgun in a side holster. The holster looked grainy like alligator or eel skin. It matched his shoes.

"You think we need that?"

"It's just a precaution."

"A precaution?"

"I'm not willing the purse yet." This was Dick's term for dying and passing on his fortune.

"Neither am I," Jerry insisted, although part of him didn't care. Perhaps if he had a wife and family. Chelsea's sister in California had tried to get chummy, but she no longer spoke to him. He refused to buy her a waterfront condominium in Malibu. To most people, he'd be more use dead than alive.

"What's the plan?" Jerry asked.

"We're having a talk."

"A talk?"

"We're his only friends. He just doesn't know it yet."

"Let's make that point clear before he shows us what he bought at the army-navy store."

When they reached Willie's house on the beach, Tom parked the Lincoln along the boardwalk. The rain stopped, and the wet sand appeared brown and dimpled, like the spiked up infield on a baseball diamond. Foamy green waves curled into the surf. Jerry felt queasy from looking at the swells, so he turned away.

"I'm staying in the car," Tom announced.

Dick's psycho-mumbo-jumbo vanished in the salt air, as he adopted a firmer tone. "You're coming with us, dough boy."

"Somebody's got to watch the car."

"Put on the alarm and get ready to head out."

Tucker nudged Tom. Begrudgingly, Tom yanked the keys from the ignition and sighed.

Jerry studied the exchange. Dick appeared too itchy to solve the world's problems. This intervention served Dick as much as Willie Nelson. Jerry hoped that one of them learned a lesson tonight. "Let's get going, before Dick empties his gun right here on the boardwalk."

Willie Nelson owned a Victorian mansion overlooking the Atlantic Ocean. Once a glorious hotel, Willie bought the place, closed the doors, and occupied the top floor with his wife. That was the balance of the Alliance files. They walked into this blind, except for Dick's and Tucker's handguns and the twenty or so rifles stashed somewhere in Willie's thirty room seaside manor. Talk about bad ideas, but Jerry kept moving forward because he hadn't heard a better one in years.

They spoke to Willie through a video monitor above the door. His face looked covered with razor stubble, like the real Willie, but beyond that, the comparison stopped. Jerry felt strange judging a man by what he wasn't.

Dick assumed the lead. "Good evening, Mr. Nelson."

"What do you want?" Willie barked.

"We need to talk."

"Did my wife send you?"

"Is she home?"

"Very funny."

"I assure you this isn't a joke."

"Are you playing games with me? What is it you want?"

The dialogue stalled. A pair of seagulls squawked overhead. The waves crashed the surf, and the breeze tousled Jerry's hair. The air smelled like rotten clams.

Dick reached into his pocket and held up a magazine article about the Winners Circle. It showed a picture of Dick standing outside the JCC. "We don't want your money."

"No?"

"The last thing we need is more cash." Dick wasn't speaking for Tom of course.

A moment later, the door buzzed open.

"Take the elevator to the top," Willie said.

The Alliance spread out in the compartment, and when the doors parted, Willie sat with a low caliber rifle across his lap. The blue steel barrel and stained wood blended with the earthy decor. Red velvet covered the walls, and an eclectic array of leather chairs and brass floor lamps dominated the floor. The exception was the electronics. Digital audio and video equipment filled an entire wall, glowing in the dimly lit room with subtle accuracy.

Jerry reached for the button to go down, but Willie seized the elevator by remote control. He pointed the black clicker in his hand, and the elevator buttons fell dark. "You may as well come in."

"I know this is unusual." Dick went first, strutting into the center of the room. Jerry never met a psychologist who didn't want to be a hostage negotiator and steal center stage.

"I know who you are." Willie rubbed the rifle barrel.

"Do you know why we're here?"

"You're from the Winners Circle."

"Correct."

"You want me to join."

"That's your choice."

"I'm out of choices."

"I assure you that things aren't that bad. We've all been in your shoes."

Willie stood up. "Is that supposed to make me feel better?"

"You're confused, but the last thing you need is to feel sorry for yourself."

"Sorry for myself? You don't know the half of it."

"Perhaps you want to tell me."

"Why? What's your game?"

Tom moved through the corner of Jerry's vision. The fidgety baker shaded himself behind Jerry, pinching his nose. He often developed a nosebleed whenever he became upset.

"Easy now." Jerry backed against the wall. He didn't want Willie getting nervous, although Tom was probably peeing his pants in private.

Tucker sucked on a toothpick. He appeared only half-interested in the rifle, checking out the stereo equipment instead. He bent over and examined the myriad buttons, knobs, and flashing lights.

Jerry imagined how things might play out: Dick gets shot at first, and then Tucker brings Willie down by reflex. Jerry counted on the Australian's cool hand. Behind Dick's mansion, he'd watched Tucker shoot the letters out of Fosters Lager cans from a good distance.

"We want to help," Dick said.

"No one wants to help." Willie's hands clenched the rifle. "Everyone wants a piece of the jackpot."

Jerry tried not to laugh but found it impossible. It was Dick's words coming right back at him.

Willie turned the rifle on Jerry. "What's your problem?"

Jerry observed the long barrel, imagining a small projectile piercing his gut. It resembled a lot of things in life. It went in small at the start and left a huge whole on the other end.

"Answer me," Willie Nelson demanded.

"Dick thinks he can help you," Jerry replied.

"What do you think?"

"I think you don't want anybody's help."

"Why did you come?"

"I came to support Dick."

Dick gave Jerry a weird glance. Willie's rifle dropped, aiming at the rug.

"The two of you need to work this out," Jerry said. "Dick wants to save you. You want to blow peoples' heads off. We have a difference of opinion."

Jerry's calm unnerved the others. He was surprised that Dick failed to recognize one of his own Winners Circle tactics. That was something else Jerry had learned about psychologists. While busy dissecting other people's problems, they rarely looked in the mirror.

"Do you know what it's like being Willie Nelson?" the namesake Willie asked, his tone bordering on rage.

"Tell me."

"It's a living hell."

Jerry cringed. *Here comes the big confession.* He'd witnessed this one hundred times at the Circle meetings. The idea of hearing another wet-eyed trip down memory lane repulsed him. But this one had a rifle, so he guessed he was going to have to listen to every word. "Go ahead."

"People laugh at you," Willie said.

"I suppose."

"They hum songs behind your back."

"I can imagine."

"Even the real Willie's miserable. The IRS hounds him every waking minute."

Jerry didn't refute it. True, both Willies were miserable.

He let the poor soul talk himself out, turning a deaf ear to the conversation. Jerry didn't give a damn what happened next. It was all over. *Pack it up. Go home. Nothing left to see here.* He expected to find Willie in room 201B at the Trenton JCC next Tuesday night. Willie would be huddled over a styrofoam coffee cup, telling stories, bitching and moaning with the rest of them.

A big screen TV droned on the electronics wall. It showed a cheery Hispanic woman, with a tad too much makeup, plucking balls from a lottery machine. Jerry checked his wristwatch. It was time for Super Pick Millions, the highlight of his day.

Four balls already sat on the chute. He recognized the numbers—a scramble of Chelsea's birthday and his own. He watched his birth month number roll down the chute.

"Nine," the woman announced, all teeth.

His adrenaline kicked up a notch. Only Chelsea's birth month remained. It sucked up the tube and rolled into view.

"Eleven," the lottery diva said.

He'd hit the Super Pick Millions numbers again and started to chuckle. "Good deal." His heels did a little dance on the carpet. He didn't even know how much money he'd won, much less if he'd have to share it with another winner.

When he spun around, he noticed the others in the room. They were watching him, each man aghast at his overt display. They peered at him as if he were crushing baby seal skulls with his boots.

Willie clutched his rifle like a spear, still tethering the trigger. "You won?"

"That's what the numbers say." Jerry stopped smirking, nonchalantly tossing his shoulders. *Of all the stupid things. I won another time.*

"Again?" Willie's voice cracked, not unlike the real Willie Nelson.

"Looks that way."

Willie charged, a crazed look in his eye. Dick stuck out his leg and tripped Willie but not before the confused millionaire squeezed the trigger by accident. The gun set off as he fell, shooting Jerry through the thigh. Jerry had even heard the shot a split second before the bullet struck. He twitched ever so slightly to the left, unable to dodge bullets as well as rattlesnakes.

Time collapsed. Jerry fell to the floor. The curse of the lottery lay upon him. It burned like a snakebite, and he laughed out loud a demonic mixture of pain and irony. This freaked out the others in the room even more than the shot.

Dick's hands shook. Tom started to cry, bunching tissues into a nostril to stem his own blood flow. Willie Nelson threw up on the oriental carpet. Only now was Tucker turning away from the elaborate controls of Willie's expensive stereo, trying to understand what had transpired.

In the back seat of the Lincoln, Jerry bled through the makeshift bandages. Crimson blood and rattlesnake venom purged from his veins, spilling onto the genuine leather seats. It was a catharsis of sorts.

"I'm sorry." Willie gripped Jerry's shoulder, apologizing like a Christian after Mardi Gras. "Jesus, I'm sorry."

Jerry listened to Willie ramble about his sad life. *Please God, don't let this be the last thing I hear.*

"I don't know what to do without her." Willie looked weepy.

"Without who?" Jerry asked. He felt dizzy.

"My wife," Willie said, finally reaching his point. "She left me three months ago."

That wasn't in the files. Jerry grabbed his saturated bandages along with Dick, but his hands were growing weak. He submerged into the twilight of consciousness.

"Get a move on it, Tom," Dick yelled.

The Navigator's engine roared like Jerry's Porsche in high gear. His life felt too dumb to be his own, but it was his. It was the life he'd let happen to him, a life by attrition.

"We were married seven years," Willie continued. "I've known her since high school. That's forever."

Jerry studied Willie's face, taking a good look at the man who shot him. He understood what made Willie so angry. He didn't blame the poor slob for anything after that.

"And you know what his name is?" Willie Nelson sobbed like a lost toddler.

"No." Jerry didn't care. He wanted to stop hemorrhaging. Suddenly he wanted to live a long time. The mundane aspects of life—breathing, hurting, laughing, crying, itemizing tax deductions—made sense as he encroached the point of release. *Alright, maybe not itemizing tax deductions.*

"Her boyfriend's name is Tony Bennett," Willie said.

"The real Tony Bennett?" Jerry asked.

It was a good thing they'd left the rifles back at the mansion. Willie looked ready to shoot Jerry on purpose this time.

CHAPTER 18

FLORENCE FRIGHTINGALE

Jerry received two blood transfusions in a forgettable south Jersey hospital. A nurse with sallow fingers swabbed his gunshot wound with sterile gauze, while a yawning surgeon phoned ahead to the operating floor. Jerry felt trapped in a nightmare. His life acquired the graininess of late night television.

"You're saying Mr. Nelson didn't intend to fire his weapon at you?" A rural police detective stood beside the emergency room gurney, flipping through the pages of his spiral notebook. He poked his large forehead with the eraser tip of a pencil. His day probably amounted to stolen bicycles and vandalized mailboxes, and he fought to make sense of the shooting.

"He didn't want to hurt anyone." Jerry examined the jagged vivisection of his leg, keeping his eyes away from the cop. He knew that much about lying. "He was showing us his rifle."

"A loaded rifle?"

"I know, not very safe."

The detective scribbled in his notebook. "Then it was an accident."

"That's what I'm saying." Jerry glanced up at the disbelieving cop. *Yup, that's my story.*

"You're certain."

Jerry refused to turn over on Willie. He understood the effects of a wife who left after you gained the means to offer her anything in the world. A bullet in the thigh and a pint or two of blood was nothing in comparison. "I'm certain."

At home, Jerry limped about the farmhouse on crutches. He visited a physical therapist three times per week. Tom drove him around, brought in food, and removed the trash. Jerry considered hiring him fulltime. The sweet baker wasn't all that different than Cortez, who endlessly roamed and guarded the property. With the proper maintenance, Tom would be loyal to the end. Tom could be Jerry's version of Tucker, except wielding a rolling pin instead of a gun.

The phone rang, and Tom barged into the living room with the cordless. "It's for you."

Jerry had his feet propped upon a pillow on the coffee table. He was reading *The Miracle at Philadelphia*. He loved US history, but more importantly, he finally had the head for it again. "Who is it?"

"She didn't say. I think she knows you."

"What makes you say that?"

"It's the sound of her voice."

Jerry scanned the pudgy shape lurking near the couch. Tom had an animal instinct. He knew when the mailman was going to arrive or the teakettle approached the boiling point. He dove into menial tasks with vigor, appearing happiest while resting in a sunny spot, licking crumbs from the corners of his mouth. Yes, he was more like Cortez than anyone thought.

The phone passed to Jerry's hands, and he looked at Tom. "Do you still have your family holed up in that apartment?"

"Yeah, why?"

"I want to speak with you before you leave."

"What about?"

"We'll talk later."

Tom shrugged his round shoulders and retreated into the kitchen. He was no doubt seeking a sleeve of crackers and a hunk of cheese.

"Congratulations." Chelsea's voice struck out over the wire. It seemed to slap Jerry in the face, making him sit up at attention.

He dropped the book in his lap. He heard himself breathe into the receiver. It sounded like the wind before the rain began.

"Jerry?" she started again. "Congratulations on winning the lottery."

"I'd given up on hearing from you."

"Oh that. I'm sorry about that."

"It doesn't matter." He gauged the joy in her voice. She presented a good front but didn't sound all that happy for him. "It wasn't as big as our pot."

"It's fourteen million dollars, Jerry. I read about it in *Time* magazine."

"Really?" He didn't believe her. She must have recognized his winning numbers in the newspaper. They were identical to their winning numbers. He never really considered the odds, but lightning had struck twice. If he ever returned to the Winners Circle, he'd let Arlene try to rationalize those odds.

"You've done it again. You're so lucky."

"Am I?"

"You're amazing."

"What's amazing?"

"You remind me of the first time. You didn't care about the money then either."

"I never did." He stopped short of explaining. He recalled how arrogant it sounded when rich people renounced their wealth without any intention of losing a penny. In truth, he'd gotten used to having a heap of cash. It made the everyday answers simple. It beat the pants off holding a regular job.

"You're not like anyone I know."

"No, I'm not." He thought about that in both good and bad ways. There weren't any simple emotions regarding Chelsea. He'd gotten used to that. "How are things on your end?"

"You know."

"Is it getting better?" He already knew the answer. Haskell (a.k.a. Melvin) was being indicted for real estate fraud. The Cogdon's were selling their custom home at the shore. The minutia of their lives played out in the public eye, and everyone was a critic. The newspapers quoted more attorneys and punsters than Jacob Johansen had chickens.

"It's getting there. Things are looking up, I think."

"Really?"

"It won't be easy. I have some decisions to make."

He wondered what she meant by that, but he was in an unusual place with her, where he didn't ask and she didn't tell. "I wish you the best."

"Thank you. I know you mean that."

He considered inviting her over but waited for the urge to pass. What would it prove? Too much time separated them. He never thought he'd feel like that. He'd cheated death twice. Neither a rattlesnake bite or a bullet was enough to conquer him, yet learning to unlove Chelsea was a more serious wound. If it didn't kill him, there'd always be something left to give. "Chelsea, can I ask you something?"

"What is it?"

"Do you ever think about before?"

The receiver went silent for a moment. "Oh Jerry, I don't know."

"I'm not just talking about us. Did things turn out like you dreamed?"

"Like I dreamed?"

"What was better—the dreams or now?"

She paused again, barely able to maintain her facade over the phone line. "Don't be so serious. Spend your money. You can do a million different things."

He nearly dropped another comment about not wanting the cash but let the issue rest at that. He decided to make a joke, still feeling responsible for lifting her spirits. It was something he could do for free. "So I'm nothing but possibilities, eh?"

She laughed, but he heard a twinge in her voice. It repelled the better part of his humor. He wondered if the conversation hit too close to home, or maybe it was only their connection from miles apart.

"I'm going to hang up now." He noticed his feet on the ground. His leg ached, and he felt dizzy, but he was standing for the first time without crutches. He held his stance for what seemed like minutes after he put down the phone.

"She's here." Tom rushed into the living room, looking pasty. He pinched his nose, groping for the tissue box. A panic nosebleed was about to start.

Jerry closed his book. Rays of yellow sunlight cut through the arching glass windows. It made the room appear as if it were aflame. "Who's here?"

"Gina."

"Spagnoli?"

"Yeah." Tom tilted back his head.

"Don't let her in."

"Too late."

Gina rounded the corner from the foyer. She was dressed in her nurses' uniform and hugged a large paper bag with one arm. "That's right. I'm here."

Jerry scanned the cute and troublesome woman. Pink barrettes clasped her hair. The soles of her pink sneakers squeaked on the hardwood floor.

"Don't get up on my account. I know what you've been through." She shuffled to the couch and fluffed a pillow behind Jerry's back.

"Gina?"

"Yes."

"What are you doing?"

"What's it look like? Fluffing."

"Why?"

"I owe you."

He clutched her hand in his big palm. "Gina."

She gazed down at him with big doe eyes. "Yes, baby."

"You don't owe me anything, alright?"

"Don't be silly. I'll make tea." She shuffled into the kitchen.

Jerry spotted Tom in the corner. "Did you forget to tell me something?"

Tom shrunk into an armchair like a tossed sack of sand. "No, I swear."

"Did she call ahead?"

"I didn't get a phone call."

"Why's she here?"

"I'm waiting for you to tell me."

"Can you ask her to leave?"

Tom shoved a wad of tissue up his nose. "Me?"

A pot crashed to the floor in the next room. The men listened to the stainless steel lid wobble on the tiles.

"Terrific. I'll do it myself." Jerry grabbed a crutch and hobbled into the kitchen.

Gina set the pot on the stove. Groceries from the bag were scattered on the countertop. "Where's your beater?"

"My what?"

She twirled a finger in the air. "The spinning thing."

"What do you want with that?"

"I use it to mash potatoes, unless you have a better way."

"You're mashing potatoes?"

"Would you prefer baked?"

"Why are we discussing potatoes?"

"You need to keep up your strength." She lifted a packaged hunk of beef from the counter. "Red meat to restore your blood."

"I had a transfusion in the hospital."

"Green beans for folic acid."

"I take vitamins."

"You're funny, Jerry."

She moved about his refurbished kitchen, a wooden spatula in her fist. She tossed the potatoes in the sink and rinsed the beans.

He watched her for a while, wondering when to introduce the idea of her departure, but he felt tired and achy. He didn't want to pop another painkiller. He hated those pills.

Jerry limped back to the couch and sat down.

Tom hadn't budged. A box of tissues bridged his lap. "Well ..."

"She's cooking."

"No kidding?"

"She's making dinner. Steak, I think."

"Primo." Tom sat up and rubbed his belly. "I was getting hungry."

Gina prepared a comfort food buffet: steak, ham, fried chicken, mashed potatoes and biscuits, red beets, and three kinds of beans. They sat at the dining room table with the good china and crystal. Jerry hadn't observed holidays in the last year, and he sat at the head of the table, mesmerized by the steaming spread and flickering candlelight. It looked like Christmas in May.

Tom dove into the biscuits and gravy, working the fork like a diesel shovel. Brown gravy smudged his chin. He was the big kid Jerry never had. "This is great."

"Thank you, Thomas." Gina hovered over Jerry, spooning food onto his plate. An insurmountable pile of grub assembled before him.

Jerry caught a whiff of Gina's rosy perfume. It mixed with the delectable scents. This could be his everyday life, he thought—if he didn't change the locks and hire a bodyguard.

"Where'd you learn to cook like this?" Tom asked.

"I have many hidden talents." She winked at Jerry. "Jerry knows a few of them."

Jerry agreed. Unfortunately, lying was one of her hidden talents. He'd never believe her sincerity, only her intentions. For Jerry, Gina's intentions would always pave another road to hell.

"You need a vacation." Gina sat down and spread a napkin across her lap. "How about somewhere warm?"

"I suppose you have a place in mind."

"One of the Islands. The Cayman Islands are nice."

Tom swallowed a bite of ham. "That sounds good."

"I can be your nursemaid on the trip."

Jerry picked up his fork and glanced the length of the table. *This is what rich men do. They collect people.* Soon he'd have a butler and a driver too. It was fate. He'd been spitting into the wind for too long. "Pass the gravy, please."

Gina popped out of her seat. "I'll get it." She hustled over with the ladle and smothered his potatoes with speckled brown sauce.

"Thanks."

"My pleasure." She waited for Jerry to sample and approve, before sitting down.

"Gina?"

"Yes, baby?" She smiled, broad and toothy, like the woman who plucked the ping-pong balls from the lottery machine. She looked happy on the outside but maybe thinking about being somewhere else. What did it matter? She had a job to do, and she was going after it with gusto.

"I appreciate this dinner."

"Thank you."

"I know you want to help."

"Of course I do."

"And if I asked you to leave, you'd probably ignore me."

"Oh baby, you don't want me to leave."

"Actually, I do."

The threesome grew quiet. The grandfather clock ticked in the living room. A woodpecker tapped the old oak tree. It was an uncomfortable moment that Jerry created. He used to avoid the mere suggestion of a painful pause, but now he commanded them.

Tom put down his fork and released a nervous laugh, and then Gina followed.

Jerry laughed last. He knew the joke was on him, but he could afford the bill this time.

A late frost warning swept over Pleasant Valley, and a chill filled the air. The house was silent with Gina gone for the evening. The trees rustled outside, and the grandfather clock marked the seconds. The only problem Jerry saw on the horizon was Gina's inevitable return. He might offer her a job but needed to stamp out the romance. He had a belly full of women that he didn't trust.

When the clock struck eleven, Tom started a small fire and poured clear booze into shot glasses. The men huddled in the big armchairs by the fire glow, sipping their drinks. It burned Jerry's throat. The scent of anise touched his nose.

"Ahhh." Tom's belt was undone, as well as his top trouser button. He balanced on the edge of his chair like Humpty Dumpty. It didn't appear that he was leaving any time soon.

"What is this stuff?"

"Ouzo."

"Never had it before."

"Be careful. I was in Greece right after I won the lottery. I got naked and ran around town. A bad scene."

"What did your wife do?"

"She slammed a shoe over my head in the morning."

"That's it?"

"'Never again,' she said."

"Sounds like a good woman."

"Yeah. She and the kids stuck with me."

"That reminds me. We need to talk."

"What about?" Tom poured more ouzo into his shot glass. He turned the bottle toward Jerry but noticed the full glass.

"I want you on fulltime."

"I've got my hands loaded with the bakery."

"You don't have a bakery."

"I'm working on it."

Jerry selected his words carefully. He didn't want Tom going away hurt. "Has the financing come through?"

Tom didn't answer. He drained his glass.

"So you honestly want to start getting up early again?" Jerry asked.

"Not really."

"Is it so bad doing odd jobs for me?"

"It's better than working with Dick. He's always bossing me around."

"That's just his way."

"He's a control freak."

"I know."

"But I don't think I can stand the commute to your place every day."

"Listen. I'm thinking about restoring the carriage house."

"That thing? It's a wreck."

"Take a good look at it. It's big enough for a four bed-room house."

"In your dreams."

"You have to imagine it restored."

"There you go again. You like fixing things up, don't you."

"I guess I do."

"Are you saying I can live here?"

"If you want. You'd have to help me maintain the grounds and whatever."

"I can't believe it."

"What can't you believe?"

"That's the nicest thing anyone's ever done for me." Tom shook his head. "Are you sure about this?"

"It's been on my mind for a while. We've been through a lot together."

Tom snorted.

"And that wife of yours," Jerry said, "she's been through more. Take it from me. Concentrate on keeping her happy."

"You know, she loves it up here."

"Then it's settled. Bring the whole family."

They stared into the huge stone fireplace. A log split and popped, and a spit of spark and ash bounced off the screen.

Jerry sipped the ouzo, deciding he really didn't like it. He thought about his phone conversation with Chelsea. He'd said the things that he should have mentioned before their separation. It hardly changed the world, only that he'd finally done it. He promised not to beat himself up too badly for his late timing. "A good woman's hard to find."

"That Gina's not a bad gal."

"Who?"

"Gina Spagnoli."

"Her again. She's determined to win the lottery."

"She's not that bad?"

"You have a short memory, Tom. That's why I like you."

"In my neighborhood, a good cook is worth her weight in gold, and she's not unpleasant on the eyes either."

"That's not what I'm looking for."

"What more do you want?"

"I've been asked that question before."

"What's the answer?"

"I don't know."

"You should know by now."

"I should." He put the glass to his lips but got a nose full of anise and alcohol. He rested the drink on the coffee table.

"You don't have to tell me if you don't want. It's not my business."

Jerry stared into the flames. He knew what he wanted. It took getting shot to find out. Bleeding in the back of Dick's car, he'd stood outside himself, saw himself like he really was. He'd wasted his life caring for other people. He'd been a crutch for his father, watching dad drown his grief for mom in cheap scotch and beer. After that, he'd dedicated his time to Chelsea's comfort, easing her fears and obsessions, but going solo taught him something that he'd never expected. He was strong enough to carry two people at once but lacked the drive to carry on alone.

"I guess I was looking for myself," he said.

"Oh boy." Tom looked away. "That's a lot harder. Good luck with that."

"I'm doing okay."

"What about Gina then?"

"What about her?"

"I can say one thing about her."

Jerry knew what Tom was thinking and didn't much want to hear it. It was sad but true.

"Don't get rid of Gina so fast." Tom drained another glass. "What else you got going?"

CHAPTER 19

JERRY'S RESTORATION

T he summer heat draped the valley, like a hot wet towel that people couldn't lift from their faces. Jerry began refurbishing the carriage house at the front of his property, this time without the camera crews and over-priced carpenters. The dilapidated structure needed to be torn down, but a Hopewell preservation society claimed the building was historic, and a militant attorney representing the NAACP asserted it was an abolitionist safe house. A court summons arrived from the county sheriff, and construction halted.

Jerry researched their claims and uncovered colonial documents. He hired an architecture firm in Philadelphia with experience in colonial restorations. He limped into a packed house at a Hopewell town meeting. The hostile audience mumbled, as he set up his presentation.

"Let me explain the history of this structure." He unveiled a scale model of the new carriage house. He planned to build it with salvaged beams, clapboards, and ornamental details from the original structure. "If we can settle down, please. We have a lot to discuss."

He assumed the center of the room. His voice shook, as he shuffled through his index cards, but he tucked them into his blazer. He knew them by heart, and his nerves began to quiet. He started speaking, his confidence expanding with each passing point.

When his presentation ended, local residents and officials fired questions for more than an hour. Jerry kept his ground, promising to hold an open house with tours on two weekends per year. He eyed the attorney stalking one side of the room. Jerry'd managed to stifle his arguments before they arose. In fact, he'd satisfied every complaint in the court summons. He'd walked into the meeting amid grumbles and jeers, and when he left, they applauded him.

He reached his car in the lot, with the leaders of the preservation society and reporters from both of the local newspapers on his heels. The same people who filed suit against him began suggesting that he take on another restoration project in town.

The Porsche awaited. He stopped beside the open car door, peering down on his former detractors. He'd stood up for himself and won. He felt like the wind that blew through the hills and valleys of Hopewell. He'd always been a part of the community but passed among them unnoticed. On this day, he had to be acknowledged.

CHAPTER 20

THE END OF THERAPY

O n his last day of physical therapy, Jerry worked the weight machines and repeated the prescribed stretches faster than ever. He was bored with the routine and had almost canceled the appointment.

The nurse shook his hand at the finish. "You'll probably always experience some pain."

"I'm anticipating it."

"Your doctor can write you a prescription."

"I don't mind the pain. I like the reminder." He offered no further elaboration, harboring the meaning of his words deep inside. *When you let other people make your decisions, you can wind up shot, broke, alone, or all three.*

He stopped at the vending machine for a bottle of water. His cell phone rang, and he flipped it open and stared into the room where the seniors exercised. Debussy played on the stereo, and grey heads of hair gently rolled back and forth to the melody.

Jerry heard a familiar voice on the phone line. "Gina?"

"It's me, baby. You want to talk?"

"I've told you a million times to stop calling me that."

"A million?"

"You like that number, don't you?"

"I can't tell if you're joking."

"You've been a great help. I want to employ you full-time."

"Employ?"

"Run some errands. Cook dinner. Like you've been do-ing."

"But you have Tom for that."

"He does the heavy work, or at least, he arranges for it to be done."

"What are you saying?"

"I'd never thought I'd say this, but you're handy to have around. I'd like to hire you."

"Hire me?!"

"You can't go on working for free."

"Work for free?"

"Gina, it's a good offer."

"What kind of girl do you think I am?!"

The affordable kind, he thought. He stifled a laugh. "You don't actually think we have a future together?"

"Of all the outrageous things to say."

"Gina?"

"Jerry Nearing, you're awful."

He heard the line disconnect, surprised that his offer had insulted her. He believed Gina was unflappable, and he chuckled. *Good deal, I should have done that a month ago.* He flicked closed the cell phone and jammed it back in his pants pocket, like a gun in a holster.

The music stopped across the hall, and the seniors gathered to chat at the head of the class. Jerry was just pulling away from the vending machines, when he saw her standing among them. He'd notice that blonde head of hair anywhere, not to mention those gorgeous legs. Chelsea still owned a direct line to his heart.

An elderly woman with powder white hair wandered from the room. She noticed Jerry staring. "That's nurse Adams."

"You mean nurse Cogdon," Jerry said.

"I'm pretty sure it's Adams."

Jerry glanced back into the room. It was Chelsea, using her maiden name once again.

"She's a real looker isn't she."

"That she is," he said instinctively.

Chelsea caught sight of him in the hall. "Jerry?"

He walked swiftly away on his rehabilitated legs, hardly limping, pretending he hadn't heard, but he forgot Chelsea was a jogger. She'd outrun him.

"Jerry?" She intercepted him by the exit.

He took a breath and faced her. He could do this. He could be cool. He manufactured every bit of charm that he'd acquired in her absence. "Yes, nurse Adams."

"I guess you heard about that."

He nodded toward the elderly lady who was still standing beside the machines. "One of your friends informed me."

"I volunteer here on Wednesdays." She wore a tightfitting tracksuit. She was still put together as well as ever.

"This is where I get physical therapy."

"I heard about your accident." She appeared to want to touch his leg, but he imagined a lot of things whenever he saw her.

"We can't seem to keep out of the newspapers."

"No, we can't."

He kicked his leg once in the air. He didn't want her sympathy. "Today's my last day. I'm good as new."

"I'm surprised I hadn't run into you sooner."

"So what's with your maiden name?"

"Then you don't know."

"Not entirely."

She glanced at the floor. "Haskell and I split up two months ago."

He wondered how he'd missed that, although he'd stopped reading the papers so closely and no longer glanced at the Winners Alliance files like Dick asked. He did the math. The last time they spoke, she was already alone. That explained her defensive attitude. Chelsea hated failure.

"It was a big mistake," she said.

Jerry let this information sink in, promising himself not to be bitter. It wasn't his style. "Chelsea Cogdon didn't have much of a ring to it anyway."

"No."

"You could've had dinner with me that night and saved yourself a trip to Mexico."

"I should have. It was stupid rushing off like that and ... rushing out on you." She caught his eyes. She echoed an old expression, one he'd savored many times before but still couldn't find words to explain, only that it was coupled to his heart.

"Well, that was a couple of dinners ago. I'm fine with it now." Jerry wasn't so sure that he'd convinced even himself.

"I'm fine too. I saved the last million, almost a million."

"Good for you."

"I figured you'd want to know that I was okay."

He did, but he didn't want to admit it, not to her, not to the love of his life who'd torn out his heart and left him for dead. "I'm sure you need to tell this to someone, but not me. I'm the last person in the world."

"Are you still angry with me?"

"That's a really stupid question."

"I'm sorry."

"It's the dumbest one I've ever heard." Jerry pushed through the door, awash in the heat and light of the midday sun. He needed to breathe again, but that damned humidity was there, suffocating him.

Chelsea latched onto his arm, stepping with him into the parking lot. Her expression changed. She looked nervous, a bit of the old quivering in her lip. Her perfected face was unmasked, exposing a glimmer of the girl from Chesterfield. "You were right."

This admission rocked him. He felt every one of her fingers gripping his arm, every print upon his bicep. He'd never seen her this vulnerable. Why was she doing this? Why? "I was right about what?"

"The dreams," she said.

"What dreams?"

"Our dreams. It was better before when we dreamed."

He yanked his arm free and stared at her. They were both naked beneath the sun. The sensory points on his body burned at the surface. He'd wanted the truth from her for so long, and now he didn't want it. He wanted to give it back, let her bury the useless facts forever. "I would've spent my last million to convince you sooner."

"I know," he thought he heard her say, as he turned and left her.

Jerry Nearing hardly drove the Porsche. He worked the clutch and turned the wheel, but it seemed to propel forward under its own command. He kept replaying the conversation with Chelsea. Why apologize now? He swallowed every bit of it down deep, and only by luck, he didn't plow into a tree along the roadside.

Before he realized, he was cruising past Taddler's Horse Center. A heap of manure rose behind the main barn. It was the largest pile he'd seen there. It made him realize how his life's aspirations had transformed into crap. He saw the simplicity in that and accepted it as a sign. He directed his Porsche onto the property.

He parked beside the pile and rose out of his car. A familiar ferment—sweet, earthy, repugnant—tickled his nose. There were times on his farm when he believed he smelled it from miles in the distance. He'd always be one step away from this line of work, no matter how full his pockets were. It was okay. He understood his anointed place in the universe.

"It's a mess." Sam Taddler approached Jerry in jeans and a dirty denim shirt with a designer logo. He wore riding boots, but Jerry didn't remember ever seeing him on horseback.

"Morning, Sam."

"What brings you here?"

"I saw the pile."

Sam shook his head. "It's not like when you used to manage it. This guy shows up whenever he feels like."

"Why don't you let him go?"

"I fired two in the last year. What's so hard about this job? A monkey could do it." Sam gave Jerry a double take. "Sorry. I didn't mean anything by that."

"No offense."

"It's just hard to find men of your reliability."

Big Jerry Nearing folded his hands behind his belt. He felt the sun on his neck and shoulders. He saw horses galloping in the paddock. The land spread away from the tall black and white barn where men lowered hay from the loft and splashed hoses into the troughs. Taddler's impressed him. The entire operation was real and honest work, something he looked forward to seeing, even just passing it on the road. "You want me to take care of this pile?"

"You?"

"Yes."

"What do you want with it?"

"Same as before. I can sell it around the county."

"Are you crazy?"

"I've never felt better."

Sam laughed out loud. "You're pulling my leg."

"No, sir."

"What's up?"

"You're going to teach me how to ride a horse."

Sam scratched his head. "You want lessons? I can sell you those."

"I want to learn how to teach others. That's what I really need to know."

"You're going to buy horses, aren't you."

"I'm thinking about it."

Sam laughed again. "You're not crazy."

"No, I'm past that."

"Alright then. Come sit with me in the office. I'll show you a little of this business and see if I can't change your mind."

"I don't see that happening."

"Maybe we can work something out."

"I'd like that."

Sam took a few steps with Jerry, before turning toward him. "I still need for you to get this horseshit out of here."

"No problem. I'm your man."

CHAPTER 21

SAVING MERCER OAK

A week passed, and no one showed at the farm. Every time the phone rang or someone arrived at the door, Jerry expected to hear Gina Spagnoli or find Dick Leigh's stare hovering above the stoop, but it didn't happen.

When word finally came, Jerry received a simple unmarked telegram. He squinted at the brief message.

MEET ME AT MERCER OAK – 3:00PM

Of all the places to choose. Gina was the only woman he'd told about his special place with Chelsea. That woman had nerve.

But he recalled Chelsea at the therapy center and her fragile confession. It'd been working the back of his mind for days, and the telegram stirred it up again. Could it be her? She'd never actually finished speaking, told her whole story. As a couple, they'd thrived by silent contracts and unspoken dialogues. Her apologies arose as earnest gestures and shrouded phrases, but at the therapy center, under the blinding sun, she was trying to explain herself for the first time, and he couldn't wait to get away from her. He had cut her short.

He gripped the telegram in his hand and shook off the possibility of something more. No, he was going to let Chelsea apologize, and that was it. He was strong enough to stand for it, although he realized that he'd been avoiding this day too. It was easier to be angry, to stay ever-longing, than to kiss the dream good-bye for good.

The Porsche raced toward Battlefield Park. Jerry's fists clenched the steering wheel. The closer he drove to Princeton, the more he was certain it was Chelsea's telegram—so like her not to sign her name, so like her to hide in matters of the heart. She was scared—an emotion that reached all the way to the beginning, as if she was asking for shelter once again.

Red lights flashed in Jerry's rearview mirror. He glanced at the speedometer. *Too fast for this town.*

Jerry pulled into the road shoulder along Mercer Street and stopped near the edge of the park.

The officer rose out of his squad car and ambled toward Jerry's window. It took a moment for Jerry to recognize him. It was the senior officer who'd arrested him on the afternoon that Mercer Oak split and tumbled.

Jerry sank in the seat. He caught a glimpse of the cop's handcuffs reflecting in the sun.

"Good day, Mr. Nearing." A distinct sound of resignation echoed in the officer's voice—part apathy, part surrender, as if every word offered a sigh.

"Hello." Jerry had his driver's license and registration in his hand. He poked them out the window.

"I know who you are," the officer said but accepted the paperwork anyway.

"Yes."

"It's a little fast, don't you think?"

"I wasn't paying attention." He squinted into the park from far away. Kids played baseball. Someone flew a kite. The amputated hulk of Mercer Oak was surrounded by yellow police tape. He strained for a glimpse of Chelsea, to no avail.

"In a hurry?"

"Not particularly."

The officer seemed to sense Jerry's anxiety. He glanced down the road. "What is it with you and that tree?"

"Excuse me?"

"You seem like a decent man. I saw in the paper how you're restoring that historic house, but I don't get this."

"What don't you get?"

"You and that tree. What's the attraction? It's a stump."

"It's not the tree exactly."

"Oh it's the tree."

"Well ..."

"I've seen protests around it. Famous tree surgeons have tried to save it. They've even shot movies there."

"I know about all that."

"Then there's you. I can't figure you out."

"It's a long story." Jerry stared down the road.

"I'm not sure I want to hear it."

"Then you better write me a ticket if you want to get home in time for dinner."

The men didn't speak. Jerry heard a small plane pass overhead.

The officer handed back Jerry's license and registration. "Here's what I'm going to do. I'll give you a warning this time."

"Thank you." Jerry hardly believed he was getting off.

"You have to make me a promise."

"Anything you say?"

"First, you'll have to slow down."

"I can do that." No doubt, relief washed across his face. One more violation, and he'd lose his driver's license.

"Second, something tells me that you're headed toward that tree."

"You're right."

"Promise me when you get there that I won't have to arrest you again."

"You won't."

"I hope not."

Jerry grabbed the stick shift. "Thanks."

The officer tilted his chin, leery of making a grave error. "Don't make a fool out of me."

"Never." Jerry dropped the car in gear and eased away like a ninety-year-old grandmother out for a drive.

He cruised another quarter mile and parked beside the Mercer Oak. It looked hideous up close, split, truncated, but somehow right for the occasion. An expert was supposedly replanting a section of the original tree, but there was nothing there that Jerry believed salvageable, only hopes gone awry.

The air was splendid, eighty degrees and unusually low humidity, a rare New Jersey summer afternoon without threatening rain. Jerry walked onto the grass, searching for a woman he'd recognize any place on Earth. He slid on a pair of sunglasses.

He rounded the tree, seeing the edge of a silver ice bucket and a pair of sandals cast shy of bare feet. He was lifted by his luck with the police officer and decided to sit with Chelsea and make peace with her again, at least try.

He saw her long legs and picked up the pace. A familiar body assembled from the legs to the thighs, and then hips. Chelsea Adams wore a short black dress and the string of pearls left behind by his mother. He stopped walking. This wasn't a mistake. She'd done this on purpose. A woman presented herself like this before a man to either love him or kill him, perhaps a little of both.

"I didn't know if you'd come," she said.

"I guessed it was you." He'd heard the uncertainty in her voice. It wasn't all that different than the first time they'd made love. He gave her credit. She had guts to go through with a risky plan.

She stretched her legs and crossed her ankles, but she didn't appear entirely comfortable. He recognized the tension in her feet—an exaggerated arch in her foot. He wondered if he'd caused it to appear. He'd frozen at the sight of her. What was his body language saying? His hands were jammed in his pockets. His knees felt shaky. He wanted to move, but in which direction?

"I thought of writing a letter," she said.

"You sent a telegram."

"I'm serious."

"What would the letter say?"

"I'm sorry."

"What are you sorry for?"

"All of it. You knew better." She looked down and batted her eyes. She was embarrassed, but it was real emotion, like the last time they'd met. It was wonderful to see. "When did you get so much smarter than me?"

"From a lifetime of watching you."

"What did you see?"

"You're asking me now?"

"I bet you saw a woman running from herself."

"Yeah, I saw that, but you wound up running from the parts I liked the best." He heard himself fashion confessions when he'd come to only listen to hers, but another part of him knew that he wouldn't have been able to speak so frankly just one year ago. "And did it work? Did you get away from yourself?"

"Like you said, just the best parts."

"Not entirely."

"You said it. You tried to warn me, but I didn't listen."

Even now, he wasn't comfortable with her speaking like this. In his old-fashioned sense of men and women, he wanted to be loved by the best, and if he held any chance of grabbing what he thought Chelsea was offering, he wasn't going to knock the girl down further. "I wasn't totally honest either. I've been angry with you for a while."

She nodded. "How did we end up like this?"

"I can give you a million, no, thirty-two million reasons."

She pursed her lips. "But you've changed too."

He took off his sunglasses and tucked them in his shirt pocket. "It's still me."

"You're different."

"How so?"

"You're everything I always thought you'd be."

He read her apology in between the lines. She'd never be any good at it. She was the type who'd rather thrust herself into a solution to fix things, and she was doing this now.

The sky was filled with puffy white clouds, like the smoky remnants of fireworks blasts. Jerry watched them drift past. All he ever wanted to do was make her happy. "It's amazing what a change of clothes will do for a man."

The dimple pooled in her cheek. She smoothed her skirt with her hands. "I tried to explain myself over the phone."

"You didn't explain much."

"See what I mean? I've wanted to call you for months, even before Haskell and I split up, but you made it hard."

"There you go mentioning Melvin's name." He hated that she'd slept with Cogdon. That was a hurdle to jump, but he squelched those feelings. He'd have to work them out. In truth, he'd slept with more strange women than she did men in their time apart, and whatever it was that she saw when she peered at him, she'd returned for more. She'd come home.

"You've developed a sharp sense of humor," she said.

"You have to laugh at us millionaires."

She looked away, verging on tears. "You must hate me."

"For some reason, you hated yourself even more." He saw her ashamed. It never occurred to him that she understood she was wrong for a long time. Chelsea was always right. She never screwed up. At least, that's how events usually passed between them.

Jerry saw the moment where he should stay or go. It was as if a line formed in the grass: step over it or retreat. The choice might be hard for some men weakened by vanity or pride, but he knew what he'd do. It was the easiest step he'd taken in the last two years. He sat beside her, confident he had nothing to lose. "Are you paying attention to me now?"

Her ice blue eyes came back to him. She was opened up, irresistible. The big decisions belonged to him. Things would never be the same. They'd be better, hopefully stronger. Some people went to therapy to reach this point. Hell, he'd done that and almost gotten killed.

He noticed a bottle of wine and two glasses in the ice bucket. "You were pretty sure of yourself."

"I didn't know if … I wanted to be …" She swallowed a lump in her throat. "I don't know what I want to say."

He liked that she wasn't so certain. He poured the wine and gazed at the sky. The clouds drifted slower than time.

She brought the glass to her sculpted lips. That was the hardest part of her to reconcile. "I hope we don't get in trouble for this."

"Hey, I've been arrested here before. It's no big deal."

"No, really."

"Don't worry. I think we've been in enough trouble to last a lifetime." He threw an arm over her waist and pulled her close, kissing her for all time in broad daylight. There was no way on this planet that he was letting her make the first move, and she was not a woman who was about to argue.

CHAPTER 22

HOPEWELL, HEAVEN

Jerry stabbed his pitchfork into a pile of horse manure behind Taddler's main barn. Chelsea was at the farmhouse, nibbling on crackers and sipping Chamomile tea. She didn't keep much down in the first trimester. Tom baked up old family specialties in the huge baker's oven at the carriage house, but nothing settled her stomach.

The crisp fall weather was on Jerry like a fast whip cracking across his bare arms, and the manure stunk to high heaven. He savored the hard labor, even though the college kids he'd hired did most of it. He felt time slipping through his fingers, but in a good way. He'd learned to ride horseback. He helped one of the mare's bare a foal at the first sight of dawn. It made him think of his own child in Chelsea's belly. Dreams are brief and immediate. You better grab them before they vanish into thin air.

And the past—the past is nothing you can settle in the present. There are only hateful words for that, like spite, bitterness, and vengeance. Jerry wasn't much for that sort of dirty work. He and Chelsea vowed to never discuss their time apart. They called it the lost years and folded it up on the shelf, like a photo album that never gets taken down to view.

Jerry released his pitchfork and turned his face to the sun. It burned through his eyelids, fiery yellow, then bright white. He didn't have to dream about Chelsea any longer. That was the best part of making her real again, yet sometimes when he looked at her, he saw a wrinkle in her upper lip, so small no one else would notice. That was the nature of their relationship. You can't make everything perfect. He knew, because together they were damn close to it.

THE END

Christopher Klim worked on observation and exploration satellites for the space program, until departing for the private sector to develop leading-edge communications technologies. He now teaches and mentors emerging writers. He is the senior editor of *Writers Notes Magazine* and primary architect of the website www.WritersNotes.com. In his lectures, writings, and workshops, this award-winning storyteller entertains with contemporary tales that extend the American experience while transcending the ordinary. His novels *Jesus Lives in Trenton* and *Everything Burns* have won critical acclaim, and his manual on the writing craft, *Write to Publish: Essentials for the Modern Fiction & Memoir Market* is preferred among writers. He's also written the praised children's novel *Firecracker Jones Is On The Case*. He lives in New Jersey.

Contact the author:
c/o Hopewell Publications
PO Box 11
Titusville, NJ 08560-0011
Author@ChristopherKlim.com

www.ChristopherKlim.com
www.Write-to-Publish.com
www.WritersNotes.com

Books by Christopher Klim

EVERYTHING BURNS
ISBN 0972690654, $15.95

A TEXAS CITY CATCHES FIRE, as photojournalist Boot Means races to stop a serial arsonist from creating his master-piece inferno. With Klim's trademark grit and stunning scenarios, he reveals the heart of a true pyromaniac.

"Absorbing reading!" – *Booklist*

"Even slicker, sexier than his last."
– *Circle Magazine*

JESUS LIVES in Trenton
ISBN 0972690603, $15.95

BIG TROUBLE COMES FOR tabloid photojournalist Boot Means. It's an exhilarating and hilarious journey into the heady world of TV evangelism and the seamy underworld of cult organizations.

"... undeniable charm." – *Booklist*

"His ear for dialogue would make Hammett proud." – *Philadelphia Weekly*

*Available at **www.ChristopherKlim.com** and better stores.*

Printed in the United States
37277LVS00005B/199-210